THEODORE
BOONE
The Activist

John
Grisham

THEODORE
BOONE

The Activist

HODDER &
STOUGHTON

First published in Great Britain in 2013 by Hodder & Stoughton
An Hachette UK company

1

Copyright © Boone & Boone, LLC 2013

The right of John Grisham to be identified as the Author of the Work has been
asserted by him in accordance with the Copyright, Designs and Patents Act 1988.

A CIP catalogue record for this title is available from the British Library.

Hardback ISBN 978 1 444 72893 4
Trade Paperback ISBN 978 1 444 72894 1

Printed and bound by Clays Ltd, St Ives plc

Hodder & Stoughton policy is to use papers that are natural, renewable
and recyclable products and made from wood grown in sustainable forests.
The logging and manufacturing processes are expected to conform to
the environmental regulations of the country of origin.

Hodder & Stoughton Ltd
338 Euston Road
London NW1 3BH

www.hodder.co.uk

THEODORE
BOONE
The Activist

Chapter 1

The opponent was the team from Central, the "other" school in town and the great rival of Strattenburg Middle School. Whenever there was a game or a match or contest of any sort against Central, the tensions were higher, the crowds were bigger, and things just seemed more important. This was true even for a debate. One month earlier, the SMS Eighth-Grade Debate Team had won at Central in a packed auditorium, and when the decision was announced by the judges the crowd was not happy. There were a few boos, though these were quickly hushed. Good behavior and sportsmanship were expected, regardless of the contest.

Strattenburg's captain was Theodore Boone, who was also the anchor, the closer, the go-to guy when the pressure was on. Theo and his team had never lost, though they were not quite undefeated. Two months earlier, they had tied with the SMS girls' team after a rowdy debate on the issue of raising the driving age from sixteen to eighteen.

But Theo wasn't thinking about other debates at the moment. He was onstage, seated at a folding table. Aaron on one side and Joey on the other, all three young men in coats and ties and looking quite snappy, and all three staring across the stage at the team from Central. Mr. Mount, Theo's adviser, friend, and debate coach, was speaking into a microphone and saying, "And now, the final statement by Strattenburg, from Theodore Boone."

Theo glanced at the crowd. His father was sitting in the front row. His mother, a busy divorce lawyer, was tied up in court and upset that she was missing her only child in action. Behind Mr. Boone was a row of girls, including April Finnemore, one of Theo's closest friends, and Hallie Kershaw, the most popular girl in the entire eighth grade. Grouped behind the girls were a bunch of teachers: Madame Monique, from Cameroon, who taught Spanish and was Theo's second favorite, after Mr. Mount, of course; and Mrs. Garman, who taught Geometry; and Mrs. Everly, who taught English. Even Mrs. Gladwell, the principal, was there. All in all a nice crowd, for a debate anyway. For a basketball or football game, there would have been twice as many spectators, but then those teams had more than three contestants per side, and, frankly, were more exciting to watch.

Theo tried not to consider these things, though it was difficult. An asthma condition prohibited him from participating in organized sports, so this was his chance to compete before spectators. He loved the fact that most of his classmates were terrified of speaking in public, while he enjoyed the challenge. Justin could dribble a basketball between his legs and hit three-pointers all day long, but when called on in class he was as timid as a four-year-old. Brian was the fastest thirteen-year-old swimmer in Strattenburg, and he enjoyed the confident swagger of a great athlete, but put him in front of a crowd and he wilted.

Not Theo. Theo spent little time in the bleachers cheering for the other kids; instead, he hung around courtrooms and watched lawyers battle before juries and judges. He would be a great lawyer one day, and though he was only thirteen, he had already learned the valuable lesson that speaking in public was important to success. It wasn't easy. In fact, as Theo stood and walked business-like to the podium, he felt his stomach flip and his heart race. He had read stories of great athletes and their pregame routines, and how many of them were so tense and edgy they would actually vomit. Theo did not feel sick to his stomach, but he felt the fear, the unease. A veteran trial lawyer had once told him: "If you're not nervous, son, then something is wrong."

Theo was certainly nervous, but he knew from experience it was only temporary. Once the game started, the butterflies disappeared. He touched the microphone, looked at the moderator, and said, "Thank you, Mr. Mount." He turned to the Central team, cleared his throat, reminded himself once again to speak clearly and slowly, and began, "Now, Mr. Bledsoe makes some valid points, especially when he argues that someone who breaks the law should not benefit from it. And that many American students who were born here and whose parents were born here cannot afford college. These arguments cannot be ignored."

Theo took a breath, then turned his attention to the spectators, though he avoided eye contact. He had learned a few tricks during his career in debate, and one of the most important was to ignore the faces in the crowd. They could be distracting. They could make you lose your train of thought. Instead, Theo looked at objects when he spoke—an empty seat on the right side, a clock in the back of the room, a window on the left side—and as he spoke he continually shifted his gaze from one to the other. This gave the clear impression that Theo was tuned in to the crowd, looking earnestly, communicating. It made him seem comfortable at the podium, something the judges always liked.

He continued: "However, children of undocumented workers—we used to call them illegal immigrants—have no choice where they are born, nor can they choose where they live. Their parents made the decision to enter, illegally, the United States, and they did so primarily because they were hungry and looking for a job. It's not fair to punish the children for what their parents did. We have students in this school, and at Central, and at every school in this district, who are not supposed to be here because their parents broke the law. But, we admit them, accept them, and our system educates them. In many cases, they are our friends."

The issue was red-hot. There was a noisy movement sweeping across the state to prohibit the children of undocumented workers from enrolling in public colleges. Those who supported the ban argued that the large number of "illegals" would (1) swamp the university system; and (2) squeeze out American students who might otherwise barely qualify for college; and (3) consume millions in tax dollars paid in by real US citizens. The Central team had done a good job making these points so far in the debate.

Theo went on, "The law requires this school system, and every school system in this state, to accept and educate all students, regardless of where they come from. If the state has to pay for the first twelve years, why then should the state be allowed to slam the doors when these students are ready for college?"

Theo had some notes scribbled on a sheet of paper in front of him on the podium, but he refused to look down. Judges loved debaters who spoke without looking down, and Theo knew he was earning points. All three of the boys from Central had relied on their notes.

He raised a finger and said, "First, it's a question of fairness. All of us have been told by our parents that they expect us to go to college. It's part of the American dream. It seems unfair, then, to pass a law that will prohibit many of our students, and many of our friends, from being admitted to college." He raised another finger. "Second, competition is always good. Mr. Bledsoe takes the position that US citizens should be given priority in college admissions because their parents were here first, even though some of these students are not as qualified as the children of undocumented workers. Shouldn't our colleges admit the best students, period? Across this state, each year there are about thirty thousand openings for incoming freshmen. Why should anyone get special consideration? If our colleges admit the best students, doesn't that make our colleges stronger? Of course it does. No one should be admitted unless he or she deserves it, just as no one should be denied based on where his or her parents were born."

Mr. Mount worked hard to suppress a grin. Theo was on a roll and he knew it. He managed to add just a trace of anger to his voice, nothing too dramatic, but the right touch that conveyed the message—*This is so obvious, how can anyone argue with me?* Mr. Mount had seen this before. Theo was moving in for the kill.

The third finger was thrust into the air as Theo said, "The final point is this . . ." He paused and took a breath and looked around the auditorium as though his final point, whatever it might be, was going to be so true and so clear that no one in the room could have any doubt. "There are many studies proving that people with college degrees have more opportunities, better jobs, and higher salaries than people without college degrees. It's a head start to a better life. And higher salaries mean higher tax revenues, which leads to better schools and better colleges. People who are denied the chance to go to college are more likely to become unemployed, and that leads to all sorts of problems."

Theo paused again and slowly checked the top button of his jacket. He knew the button was okay, but he needed to convey the image of utmost confidence. "In closing, this notion of slamming the doors of our colleges to students whose parents came here illegally is a bad idea. It's been rejected by over twenty states already. That's why the Justice Department in Washington has promised to file a lawsuit in this state if such a law is passed. It is short-sighted, mean-spirited, and simply not fair. This is the land of opportunity, and at one time or another all of our ancestors came here as immigrants. We are a nation of immigrants. Thank you."

Mr. Mount appeared at the edge of the stage as Theo returned to his seat. Mr. Mount smiled and said, "Let's have a nice round of applause for both teams." The audience, which had been warned against expressing support or opposition in any way, offered a warm round of applause.

"Let's take a short break," Mr. Mount said. Theo, Aaron, and Joey quickly stood and walked across the stage, where they shook hands with the Central team. All six boys were relieved the pressure was finally off. Theo nodded to his father, who gave him a thumbs-up. Great job.

Minutes later, the judges announced the winner.

Chapter 2

The necktie and jacket were gone, and Theo was somewhat more comfortable in his usual khakis, though the button-down white-collared shirt was a bit too dressy. Classes were over; the final bell had sounded, and on this Wednesday Theo made his way to the band hall for a little after-school activity. Along the way, several eighth graders congratulated him on another fine performance. Theo smiled and took it all in stride as if it were no big deal, but deep inside he was quite pleased with himself. He was savoring another victory, but doing so without being cocky. "Don't ever get the bighead," a veteran trial lawyer had once told him. "Because the next jury can break your heart." Or, the next debate could be a disaster.

He entered the large band hall and went to a smaller rehearsal room where a few students were unpacking instruments and preparing for a class. April Finnemore was inspecting her violin when Theo approached. "Great job," she said softly. April rarely spoke loud enough for anyone else to hear. "You were the best."

"Thanks. And thanks for being there. It was a nice crowd."

"You're going to be a great lawyer, Theo."

"That's the plan. Not sure where music fits in."

"Music fits in everywhere," she said.

"If you say so." Theo opened a large case and carefully pulled out a cello, one that belonged to the school. April and a few of the other students owned their instruments. Others, like Theo, were still renting because they were not sure if this music thing was going to last. Theo was in the class because April talked him into it, and because his mother loved the idea of her son learning to play an instrument.

Why the cello? Theo wasn't sure, nor could he remember why he'd chosen the instrument. In fact, he wasn't sure he'd actually made the decision himself. In a string orchestra there are several violins and violas, a large bass, at least one cello, and usually a piano. The girls seemed to prefer the violins and violas, and Drake Brown grabbed the bulky bass. There was no one to play the cello. Theo knew from the moment he first held it that he would never learn to play it well.

The class was a last-minute addition to the current six-week schedule, and it was billed as a beginners' class for kids who couldn't play an instrument. Real beginners, raw beginners, students with little in the way of musical backgrounds and even less in the way of talent. Theo fit in perfectly, as did most of the kids. It was a low-pressure, one-hour class once a week and designed primarily for fun with a little instruction thrown in.

The fun was provided by the teacher, Mr. Sasstrunk, a spry little old man with long gray hair, wild brown eyes, several nervous twitches, and the same faded brown-plaid jacket each week. He claimed to have conducted several orchestras over his long career, and he had been teaching music at Stratten College for the past decade. He had a great sense of humor and laughed at the kids when they made mistakes, which happened constantly. His job, he said, was simply to introduce them to music, to just "give them a taste of it." He had no dreams of turning them into real musicians. "Let's just learn some basics here, kids, do a little practicing, and see where we go," he said each week. After four sessions the kids were not only enjoying the class, they were actually becoming more serious about their music.

All that was about to change.

Mr. Sasstruck was ten minutes late, and when he entered the rehearsal room he looked tired and worried. His usual smile was gone. He looked at the kids as if he wasn't sure what to say, then began, "I've just left the principal's office, and it looks as though I've been fired."

There were about a dozen students, and they glanced at one another with uncertainty. Mr. Sasstrunk looked as though he might start crying. He continued, "As it has just been explained to me, the city's schools are being forced to make a series of cutbacks for budget reasons. Seems as though there's not as much money as they expected, so some of the less important classes and programs are being eliminated, immediately. I'm sorry, kids, but this class has just been canceled. It's over."

The students were too stunned to speak. Not only were they upset over losing a class they enjoyed, but they also felt sorry for Mr. Sasstrunk. In one of the earlier sessions, he had joked about saving the small salary the school was paying to finish his CD collection of the works of the greatest composers.

"This doesn't seem fair," said Drake Brown. "Why do they start a class if they can't finish it?"

Mr. Sasstrunk had no answers. He replied, "You'll have to ask someone else."

"Don't you have a contract?" Theo asked, then immediately wished he'd said nothing. Whether or not Mr. Sasstrunk had a contract was none of Theo's business. However, Theo knew that every teacher in the city school system signed a one-year contract. Mr. Mount had explained it in Government class.

Mr. Sasstrunk managed a grunt and a grin and said, "Sure, but it's not much of one. It plainly states the school can cancel the class at any time for any valid reason. That's pretty typical."

"Not much of a contract," Theo mumbled.

"No, it's not. I'm sorry, kids. I guess class is over. I've really enjoyed myself here, and I wish you the best. A few of you have some talent, a few do not, but, as I've said, all of you have the ability to learn to play with hard work and practice. Remember, with practice anything is possible. Good luck." And with that, Mr. Sasstrunk slowly and sadly turned away and walked out of the room.

The door closed quietly, and for a few seconds the students stared at it in silence. Finally, April said, "Do something, Theo. This is not fair."

Theo was standing. "Let's go see Mrs. Gladwell. All of us. We'll take over her office, and we won't leave until she meets with us."

"Great idea."

They followed Theo from the room and marched as a group out of the band hall, across a foyer, outside through a courtyard, into the main building, down a long hallway, and finally into the central lobby where the principal's office was located near the doors of the school's front entrance. They marched inside and stopped at the desk of Miss Gloria, the school's secretary. One of her many jobs was to guard the door that led to Mrs. Gladwell's inner office. Theo knew Miss Gloria well, and he had once given her advice when her brother got caught driving while drunk.

"Good afternoon," Miss Gloria said as she peeked over the reading glasses on the tip of her nose. She had been typing away and seemed a bit irritated by the fact that suddenly a dozen angry eighth graders were in front of her desk.

"Hi, Miss Gloria," Theo said without a smile. "We'd like to see Mrs. Gladwell."

"What's the problem?"

So typical of Miss Gloria. Always wanting to know your business before you could discuss your business with Mrs. Gladwell. She had a reputation for being the nosiest person in the school. Theo knew from experience Miss

Gloria would find out sooner or later what the kids were up to, so he knew how to play the game.

"We were in Mr. Sasstrunk's music class," he explained. "The one that just got axed by the school, and we want to talk to Mrs. Gladwell about it."

Miss Gloria arched her eyebrows as if this simply wasn't possible. "She's busy, in a very important meeting." As she said this she nodded to the door of Mrs. Gladwell's office. It was closed, of course, as always. Theo had been in there many times, usually for good meetings but occasionally for something not so pleasant. Just last month he'd been in a fight, his only fight since the third grade, and he and Mrs. Gladwell had discussed it behind that closed door.

"We'll wait," he said.

"She's very busy."

"She's always busy. Please tell her we're here."

"I can't interrupt."

"Okay then, we'll wait." Theo looked around the large reception room. There were a couple of benches and an assortment of well-used chairs. "In here," he said, and his classmates immediately took over the benches and chairs. Those who could not find a place simply sat on the floor.

Miss Gloria was known to have grumpy moods, and evidently she was in the middle of one. She did not like the fact that her space had been invaded by a bunch of unhappy students. "Theo," she said rudely, "I suggest you and your friends wait outside in the front lobby."

"What's wrong with waiting in here?" Theo shot back.

"I said to wait out there," she replied, suddenly angry and raising her voice.

"Who says we can't wait in the school office?"

Miss Gloria's face turned red, and she seemed ready to explode. Wisely, she bit her tongue and took a deep breath. She had no right to order the kids out of the reception area, and she knew Theo knew this. She also knew Theo's mother and father were respected lawyers who did not hesitate to defend their son against adults when the adults were wrong and Theo was right. Mrs. Boone, in particular, could get rather firm when Theo took a stand against unfairness.

"Very well," she said. "Just keep it quiet. I have work to do."

"Thank you," Theo said. And he almost added that they had yet to make a sound, but he let it pass. He'd won this brief little battle; no sense in causing more trouble.

For five minutes they watched Miss Gloria as she tried to appear busy. But it was almost 4:00 p.m., and school had been out for half an hour. The day was quickly winding down. A few minutes later, the door to Mrs. Gladwell's office opened and two young parents stepped out. They barely glanced at Theo and his gang as they hurried away, obviously not happy about the meeting. Mrs. Gladwell stepped into the reception area, saw the crowd, and said, "Theo, nice job today in the debate."

"Thank you."

"What's going on here?"

"Well, Mrs. Gladwell, this is what's left of Mr. Sasstrunk's music class, and we'd like to know why the class has been canceled."

She sighed and smiled, then patiently said, "Can't say I'm really surprised. Please step inside." The students filed into her office, with Theo bringing up the rear. As he closed the door, he couldn't help but flash a nasty grin at Miss Gloria, who was watching. To her credit, she returned the smile.

Inside, the students all stood in front of Mrs. Gladwell's desk. There were only three chairs for guests, and no one was bold enough to sit down. Mrs. Gladwell understood this. "Thank you for stopping by, kids, and I'm very sorry about the music class," she said as she picked up a report of some kind. "This is a memo I received this morning from the main office of the city school administration. It came directly from Mr. Otis McCord, the superintendent, the number one man and my boss. The school board met last night in a special meeting to address the rather urgent budget problems. It seems as though the Strattenburg city school system will receive about a million dollars less than what had been promised from the city, the county, and the state. All three contribute to the school's budget, and for several reasons the funding has been reduced. So, cuts have to be made. Throughout the city, part-time teachers are being laid off. Field trips are being canceled. After-school programs, such as Mr. Sasstrunk's music class, are being cut. And the list goes on and on. It's very unpleasant, but I have no control over it."

Mrs. Gladwell had a wonderful way of making things clear. The kids absorbed every word as it became obvious that there was nothing they could do.

"What happened to the funding?" Theo asked.

"That's a difficult question. Some people blame it on the recession and tough economic times. Tax collections are down, and so there's not as much money to go around. Other people claim the school system wastes too much money, especially at the home office. I really don't know. My job is to follow orders. In addition to this music class, I have to eliminate one janitor, two cafeteria workers, four part-time coaches, as well as six other after-school classes. And, I've just told Mr. Pearce that his seventh-grade science class cannot take the annual trip to the Rustenburg Nuclear Plant."

"That's awful," Susan said. "That's a great trip."

"I know, I know. Mr. Pearce has been doing it for years."

"It doesn't seem fair to give a guy a contract, a promise, then yank it away in the middle of the course," Theo said.

"No, it doesn't seem fair, Theo. But, I'm not in charge of contracts. There's a lawyer in the home office who handles these things."

Several of the students looked at each other as reality settled in.

Mrs. Gladwell said, "I'm very sorry. I wish there was something I could do, but it's out of my hands. I'm sure Mr. McCord and the school board will hear a lot of complaints, and you're free to join in." After a long pause, she said, "Now, if there's nothing else, I have a meeting to attend."

"Thanks for listening, Mrs. Gladwell," Theo said.

"That's my job."

Defeated, the students filed somberly out of the office.

Chapter 3

Since before Theo was born, his parents had worked together in a little law firm called Boone & Boone. Their offices were in a converted old house on a quiet and shady street lined with similar offices, just a few blocks from Main Street and downtown Strattenburg. When the weather was nice, lawyers were often seen walking along the sidewalks of Park Street with their briefcases on the way to and from the courthouse, which was only ten minutes away. And during the noon hour there were packs of lawyers and accountants and architects strolling along, talking and laughing as they headed to lunch. Secretaries and paralegals were often seen scurrying about delivering important papers to other offices or hustling off to the courthouse.

Kids on bikes were not common sights, not on Park

Street anyway. But every afternoon during the week at least one—Theo—came flying along.

To his knowledge, Theodore Boone was the only thirteen-year-old in town with his own law office. It wasn't much of an office—just a tiny room at the rear of his parents' building with a door that opened onto a small gravel parking lot used by his parents and the other members of the law firm. Law offices never have enough storage room because lawyers are mentally unable to throw stuff away—and they create an enormous amount of paperwork—and Theo's office had once been used to store old files, along with cleaning supplies. Once he took over and cleared the space, he installed a card table as his desk. In the attic, he found an abandoned swivel chair that he held together with wire and superglue. On one wall there was a poster promoting the Minnesota Twins, his team, and on another wall there was a large cartoonish drawing of Theo that had been given to him on his twelfth birthday by April Finnemore.

On his desk he usually kept notebooks and school supplies, and under it there was usually a dog—Judge. No one would ever know Judge's age or where he came from, except that he came from the dog pound and was once within twenty-four hours of being put to sleep, forever. Theo had rescued him in Animal Court two years earlier, gave him a new name, and took him home, where he slept peacefully through the night under Theo's bed. During the day, Judge roamed quietly through the rooms and offices of Boone & Boone, occasionally napping on a small bed under Elsa's desk near the front door, or under the large conference table if the lawyers weren't using it, or hanging out in the small kitchen in hopes someone might drop some food. Judge weighed forty pounds, and though he ate human food, he never gained an ounce, according to the vet who saw him every four months. Judge preferred saltier foods—chips and crackers and sandwiches with meat—but he rejected almost nothing. When there was a birthday he expected cake. If someone, usually Theo, made a run to Guff's Frozen Yogurt, Judge expected his own scoop, preferably vanilla. And Judge was perhaps the only member of the law firm able to choke down the dreadful oatmeal cookies brought in at least one dark day each month by Dorothy, Mr. Boone's secretary.

About the only food Judge did not like was dog food. He preferred to eat what Theo ate, which was Cheerios for breakfast with whole milk, not skim, then whatever the rest of the family had for dinner, with a few random office snacks thrown in during the day while Theo was at school.

Because he was surrounded by lawyers, Judge knew that time was important. Appointments, conferences, court dates, meetings, schedules, and so on. Every member of the firm kept an eye on the clock, and the clock seemed to rule everything. Judge had his own clock, and he knew that on Wednesdays, as on most days, Theo arrived after school around 4:00 p.m. For this reason, Judge parked himself under Elsa's desk promptly at 3:30 and went back to sleep. But it was dog sleep, the kind that's not too deep, more of a light nap with the eyes half open and the ears listening and waiting for the sound of Theo bouncing up the front steps and securing his bike on the front porch.

When Judge heard these sounds, he stood and began to stretch as if he hadn't moved for hours, then waited with great anticipation.

Theo came in the front door with his backpack and said, "Hello Elsa," the same thing he said every day. Elsa jumped up and pinched his cheek and asked him how his day had been. Just okay. She straightened his button-down collar and said, "Your father said you were outstanding during the debate, is that so?"

"I guess," he said. "We won." Judge by now was at Theo's feet, tail wagging, waiting to be rubbed on the head and spoken to.

"You look so cute in a real shirt," she said. Theo was expecting this because he was usually greeted by some comment dealing with his wardrobe. Elsa was older than his parents, but she dressed like a twenty-year-old with strange tastes. She was also like a grandmother to Theo, a very important person in his life.

Theo spoke to his dog and rubbed his head and asked, "Is Mom in?"

"She is and she is expecting you," Elsa gushed. The woman had incredible energy. "And she is very disappointed she missed the debate, Theo."

"No big deal. She does have a job, you know?"

"Yes she does. There are some pecan brownies in the kitchen."

"Who made them?"

"Vince's girlfriend."

Theo nodded his head in approval and walked down the hall to his mother's office. The door was open and she waved him in. He took a seat and Judge plopped down beside him. Mrs. Boone was on the phone, listening. Her high-heel shoes were parked off to the side, which meant she had had a long day in court. Marcella Boone was forty-seven, a little older than the mothers of most of Theo's friends, and she believed women lawyers were still expected to dress at a higher level when they went to court. Office attire was more casual, at least for Mrs. Boone, but court dates meant a sharper outfit and high heels.

Mr. Boone, upstairs, rarely went to court and rarely cared how he looked.

"Congratulations," she said, hanging up. "Your father says you were magnificent. I'm so sorry I wasn't there, Theo."

They talked about the debate for a while, with Theo detailing the good points made by the team from Central and the counterpoints made by his side. After a few minutes, though, his mother detected something else. Theo was often amazed at how his mother could sense something was wrong. Often when he tried to play a joke on her, or fool her with some silly gag, he got nowhere. She could look at his face and know exactly what he was thinking.

"What's the matter, Theo?" she asked.

"Well, you can forget about me and the cello," he said, then told the story of the music class that no longer existed. "It doesn't seem fair," Theo said. "Mr. Sasstrunk was a great teacher. He was excited about the class, and I think he needed the extra money."

"That's awful, Theo."

"We talked to Mrs. Gladwell, and she explained all the budget cuts that have been ordered from the home office. Coaches, janitors, cafeteria workers. It's really bad and there's nothing she can do about it. She said we could complain to the school board, but if the money's not there, then the money's not there."

Mrs. Boone swung her chair around to a small sleek cabinet and began searching for a file. Upstairs, when Mr. Boone searched for a file, he simply began rummaging through the stacks of disorganized papers piled in some unknown order on top of his desk. He also kept stacks of materials under his desk, beside his desk, and it was not unusual to see documents that had simply slid off the piles and onto another spot on the floor. Mrs. Boone's office was intensely modern and neat, with nothing out of place. Mr. Boone's was old, creaky, saggy, and a mess. However, as Theo had witnessed many times, Mr. Boone could find a file almost as quickly as his wife.

She swung back around to her desk and looked at some paperwork. "This young woman came in last week for a divorce. Very sad. She's twenty-four, with one small child and another on the way. She doesn't work because she's busy being a mom. Her husband is a rookie policeman here in the city, and there's only one paycheck. They are barely surviving as a family, and there's no way they can afford a split. I recommended they see a marriage counselor and get serious about working things out. She called yesterday to inform me that her husband just learned he is being laid off by the city. The mayor has ordered every department to cut their budgets by five percent across the board. We have sixty policemen, so that means three will lose their jobs. My client's husband is one of them."

"What's she going to do?" Theo asked.

"Try and hang on. I don't know. It's very sad. She told me it seems like yesterday when she was in high school and dreaming of college and a career. Now she's terrified and not sure what's going to happen."

"Did she go to college?"

"She tried, but her financial aid was cut."

"All these cuts. What's going on, Mom?"

"The economy goes up and down, Theo. When times are good, people earn more money and spend more money, and this leads directly to more taxes being paid to the city. More sales taxes, more property taxes, more—"

"I'm not sure I understand property taxes."

"Okay, it's very simple. Your father and I own this building. It is known as real property. Land and buildings are real property, whereas cars, boats, motorcycles, and trucks are known as personal property. They get taxed, too, but back to this building. Each year the city places a value on this building. It's currently valued at four hundred thousand dollars, which is a lot more than we paid for it many years ago. After the city determines the value, it applies a tax rate to that value. Last year the tax rate was about one percent, which meant about four thousand dollars in taxes. The same thing happened to our home, but homes have a slightly lower tax rate. Anyway, we paid about two thousand dollars in real property taxes on our home. As for the personal property, we have two automobiles and the taxes were about a thousand dollars. So that's seven thousand dollars we paid into the city last year."

"Where does the money go?"

"Schools get the biggest chunk, but our tax dollars also pay for such things as fire and police protection, the hospital, parks and recreation, street maintenance, garbage collection. It's a long list."

"Do you have any say in how the money is spent?"

Mrs. Boone smiled and thought for a second. "Maybe a little. Not directly, but we elect the mayor and city councilmen and in theory they're supposed to listen to us. In reality, though, we just pay the money because we have no choice, then hope for the best."

"Do you resent paying the taxes?"

Another smile at another innocent question. "Theo, no one likes to pay taxes, but at the same time we want great schools, lots of well-trained policemen and firemen, beautiful parks, the best health care at our hospitals, and so on."

"I guess seven thousand dollars a year is not that bad."

"Theo, it's seven thousand dollars just to the city. We also pay taxes to the county, the state, and Uncle Sam in Washington. And since the economy is going through a slump, all levels of government are facing budget cuts. It's not just happening here in Strattenburg."

"So things are bad all over?"

"We've seen worse. Again, it's up and down. But it seems more severe when it affects people we know, like Mr. Sasstrunk and this young client of mine. When people we know lose their jobs, then the problem is suddenly more serious."

"Does a bad economy affect good ole Boone and Boone?"

"Oh yes, especially your father's business. When people aren't buying homes and building things, the real estate business suffers. But it's not something to worry about, Theo. We've been through this many times."

"It just doesn't seem fair."

"It's not, Theo, but then no one ever said that life is fair." Her phone buzzed with a message from Elsa. "I need to take this call, Theo. I think your father would like to see you."

"Okay, Mom. What's for dinner?"

What a joke. It was Wednesday, and Wednesday always

meant Chinese carryout from the Golden Dragon. Mrs. Boone was too busy to spend time in the kitchen.

"I'm thinking of sweet-and-sour shrimp tonight," she said.

"Sounds good to me," Theo said as he and Judge got to their feet and left the office.

Chapter 4

At the last minute, Theo decided against sweet-and-sour shrimp, opting instead for crispy beef. It was one of Judge's favorites. His father got the Chinese take-out, and at precisely 7:00 p.m. the Boones took their places behind their wooden TV trays in the den and prepared to eat. Mr. Boone blessed the food with his standard "thanks-be-to-God," and the meal was on. Judge sat beside Theo's chair, waiting patiently but also ready to eat.

The remote control was in the possession of Mrs. Boone. Months earlier the family had hammered out a truce, then an agreement that rotated use of the remote each Wednesday. When one person had the remote, there could be no complaining from the other two. After a few bites and a few comments about the great debate, Mrs.

Boone finally turned on the television and began surfing aimlessly, with no destination in mind. The volume was off. The only sound was Judge scarfing down the crispy beef. If Mr. Boone or Theo had the remote, they would go straight to their favorite show, *Perry Mason* reruns. But Mrs. Boone just surfed along, not really interested in anything. She watched little TV and had always tried to keep Theo away from it.

She finally stopped at a show called *Strattenburg Today*, a badly run news recap of the hot stories in town, if in fact there were any hot stories. Usually there were not. She hit the volume, and suddenly they were looking at the plastic smiling face of their governor. The voice-over from an unseen reporter said: "Governor Waffler was in town today to announce a new plan to finally build the Red Creek Bypass, an eight-mile loop around the city that will cost two hundred million dollars and has been hotly debated for many years. Governor Waffler was joined by local business leaders and elected officials who have been pushing the bypass. He announced that he has directed his transportation secretary to make the bypass a priority and designate enough money to build it." The camera pulled back for a wide shot of the governor talking into a microphone while a crowd of serious men in suits stood behind him.

"I can't believe this," Mrs. Boone said.

"What's a bypass?" Theo asked.

She said, "Well, in this case, it's a road to nowhere that will cost at least two hundred million dollars and allow truckers to save about five minutes as they travel through Strattenburg."

Mr. Boone chimed in, "It's also a badly needed four-lane highway that will reduce the traffic jams on Battle Street."

Mrs. Boone replied, "It's also a boondoggle. Five years ago, a conservative taxpayers group, someone from your side of the street, Woods, labeled it the third-biggest waste of taxpayer money in the entire country."

Mr. Boone replied, "And a Chamber of Commerce study found that the Battle Street congestion is so bad it is choking off growth and development."

Mrs. Boone said, "Two hundred million dollars for five minutes. Unbelievable."

Mr. Boone said, "You can't stand in the way of progress."

There was a heavy pause, and Theo managed to say, "Sorry I asked."

They listened to the governor for a moment and ate in silence. Then a local state senator took the podium and began bragging about all the wonderful ways the new bypass would make life better in the city and county. He was not very impressive—short, red-faced, chubby, sort of stuffed into a bad suit—and after he thundered on for a few minutes, Mrs. Boone said, "You voted for that clown."

Mr. Boone looked guilty and could not deny the accusation.

"Did you, Dad?" Theo asked, almost in disbelief, as if he wanted to say, "How could anyone vote for a guy like this?"

"I did," his father finally admitted.

At the age of thirteen, Theo Boone had only a passing interest in politics. Much of what he saw on television told him to stay away from it altogether. He knew his mother tended to be more liberal and his father more conservative, but he had heard them insist more than once they were simply "moderates," or somewhere in the middle. After listening to some of their discussions, he had realized there was nothing simple about being a moderate. Thankfully, his parents had the good sense not to argue politics in front of Theo. They rarely argued about anything, at least not in his presence.

Innocently, Theo asked, "Where does the two hundred million dollars come from?"

His father replied, "Mainly from the state, but there is some city and county money involved, too."

Theo asked, "But if the city is cutting budgets right and left, and canceling classes and laying off policemen and janitors, how can the city spend money on this bypass?"

His mother laughed and said, "Bingo."

"The vast majority is state money," Mr. Boone said.

"But I thought the state was cutting budgets, too."

"Bingo," his mother said again, with another laugh.

"Why do you keep saying 'bingo,' Mom?" Theo asked.

"Because, Theo, you're asking all the right questions, and there are no good answers. The bypass would be a waste of money in good times or bad, doesn't matter, but to build it now when the city, county, and state are all out of money is ridiculous."

Being lawyers, neither parent was in the habit of backing down when discussing an issue. However, Theo got the impression his father's support of the bypass was not quite as strong as his mother's opposition. There was another lull in the conversation, then with perfect timing, a spokesman for the Sierra Club appeared on-screen. Mrs. Boone, firmly and proudly in control of the remote, turned up the volume. The man said, "This bypass was a rotten idea ten years ago, and it's an even worse idea now. It crosses Red Creek in two places and will harm the quality of the city's water. It will be built very close to Jackson Elementary School, so there will be twenty-five thousand vehicles a day, many of them big trucks, running right by a playground where four hundred kids are playing. Think of the noise and pollution."

Mrs. Boone increased the volume even more.

The man from the Sierra Club went on, "The environmental impact has not been carefully studied. This project is being rammed through by the politicians who get paid off by the trucking companies."

Next was another politician, and Mrs. Boone quickly muted the television.

"What's the Sierra Club?" Theo asked.

"A bunch of radical tree huggers," his father said.

"It's one of the greatest environmental groups in the world," his mother said.

"Okay," Theo said, and took a bite. Like most kids, Theo actually enjoyed these rare moments when his parents disagreed. He decided to keep the debate going. "I'm confused," he said. "If the state and city are broke, then where does the two hundred million dollars come from?"

"Ask your father," Mrs. Boone said quickly, punting the ball across the den with incredible speed and accuracy.

"They borrow it," Mr. Boone said. "Being broke never stopped the government from spending more money. If they can't find any money, they simply borrow what they want by floating bonds."

"Floating bonds?" Theo asked.

"Now you've stepped into deep water," Mrs. Boone said with another laugh.

"Yes, it's pretty complicated," Mr. Boone said. "And let's save it for another day. The important thing to understand, Theo, is that governments do not operate the way they should. Your mom and I work hard. We represent our clients. We earn fees. We spend money on salaries, office equipment, electric bills, things like that. But, we cannot spend more than we earn. It's that simple. Most families and most businesses do this, or at least they try to. Not so with governments. They all spend too much and borrow too much and waste too much."

"Don't they have to pay back the money they borrow?" Theo asked.

"In theory, yes, but it seems like they just keep putting it off on the next generation. Our generation has basically bankrupted the country, and your generation gets to pay for it."

"Gee, thanks."

"Don't mention it." Mr. Boone stuffed half an egg roll into his mouth so he would be required to chew for a long time and not be able to talk.

Thankfully, the governor was gone and the next story was about a professor at Stratten College who was upset at the low wages being paid to the janitors on campus. He had organized a protest in front of the administration building, but his crowd appeared to be nothing more than a bunch of janitors. The professor had long gray hair and earrings and spoke in a shrill voice.

"Wild Willie Webber," Mr. Boone said. "What a clown."

"Who's he?" Theo asked.

"One of our better local acts. He teaches Russian history at the college and thinks he's a Communist. Always stirring up trouble, or trying to anyway."

Of course Mrs. Boone was not about to agree. She said, "He's actually a very effective activist for a number of causes."

"What's an activist?" Theo asked. He refused to allow a new word to fly by without a definition.

Mrs. Boone thought for a second, then said, "An activist is a person who has strong feelings about an issue, or issues, and is willing to get involved to bring about change. Woods?"

Woods nodded and said, "Yep, that's close enough. I would add that an activist is usually active on several fronts. The same characters keep popping up over and over."

"I suppose," she said.

Judge had an eye on one of Mr. Boone's egg rolls, one

of the two remaining ones, but he knew his chances were slim. Instead, he went to the kitchen for a drink of water, then returned to the den, where he situated himself directly in front of Mr. Boone and stared at the egg rolls.

"Get out of the way, Judge," Mr. Boone said.

"Dad, he loves egg rolls," Theo said.

"So do I, and I'm not in the mood to share."

"He shouldn't be eating Chinese," Mrs. Boone said. It was something she said at virtually every meal when Theo started dropping food down to Judge. Both Mr. and Mrs. Boone thought it was unwise to feed a dog off the table, and they said so often, but even while they were telling Theo not to feed Judge they knew exactly what he was doing. Mr. Boone himself was known to drop a scrap or two, and if Mrs. Boone saw it she would always say, "Woods, don't feed the dog." But Woods would feed the dog whenever he wanted to, and the next day he would say to Theo, "Theo, don't feed the dog."

Strange behavior. Theo was often baffled by the things his parents said and did. For example, every night around 9:00 p.m. when his parents were reading or talking or puttering in the kitchen, Mrs. Boone would say, "Woods, it's your turn to make the coffee." Every night after dinner, Mr. Boone ground the coffee beans, poured the water, adjusted the dial on the automatic brewer, and got everything ready for the first pot that was automatically brewed at 6:00 each morning. The couple enjoyed waking up to the smell of freshly brewed coffee, though Mrs. Boone actually drank very little. Mr. Boone craved the caffeine, and for this reason he was quite happy to go about his little nightly ritual of "making the coffee." It was his job, one that he wouldn't share with anyone. The beans had to be properly measured. The water had to be at a certain level. The filter had to be a certain type. And so on. Nevertheless, every night Mrs. Boone felt the need to remind her husband, and his response was always, "Yes, dear, I'll get to it in a minute."

Mrs. Boone refused to take out the garbage. That chore belonged to Mr. Boone, or, more often, Theo. It was no big deal and Theo didn't mind it at all. But for some reason, and out of a habit that Theo was sure neither of his parents could ever explain, about twice a week he heard his father ask, "Honey, have you taken out the garbage?" To which Mrs. Boone responded every time, "No, I just painted my fingernails."

Theo had little interest in his mother's fingernails and how often she painted them, but he was almost certain she got them worked on at a salon every Friday morning. They always looked nice, as far as Theo noticed.

Why did his parents do these odd things? Theo rarely

withheld questions, but he had a hunch that some questions were better off left unasked. Perhaps some questions could not be answered. He also suspected married people settled into routines and did things so often they didn't even realize they were doing them.

As he was pondering these things, his mother asked, "Theo, did you finish your homework?" Again, Theo could count on this question at least twice every night, usually once from his mother and once from his father. They required him to finish his homework each afternoon at the office before he left for home. Theo was a good student and could usually knock out his homework in sixty to ninety minutes, and any leftovers could be cleaned up during study hall the following day.

"Yes ma'am," he said. "All done."

"When is the next debate?" she asked.

"I'm not sure."

"I'm not going to miss it, Theo, I promise."

"You want to watch today's debate? I have it on a CD."

Mrs. Boone smiled and dropped her chopsticks. "Excellent, Theo! Pop it in."

"Great idea," said Mr. Boone, anxious to get away from the bypass issue.

Theo removed the CD from his backpack and inserted

it in the player. For the next hour, they watched Theo, Joey, and Aaron battle the team from Central and debate the pros and cons of allowing the children of undocumented workers to attend the public colleges of this state. Mrs. Boone could not stop smiling. His parents were so proud. Theo had to admit it was a good performance.

Even Judge was glued to the screen, unable to figure out how Theo could be in two places at the same time.

Chapter 5

Major Ludwig ran Boy Scout Troop 1440 like an elite Marine unit getting ready for battle. He expected his forty or so Scouts to attend both meetings each month and to come prepared, and he expected them to dress in proper uniforms. He led them, pushed them, encouraged them, and occasionally he had to discipline them. But his bark was worse than his bite, and the Major at heart was a soft touch. The boys admired him greatly and did not want to disappoint him. Theo had been a member of the troop for two years and was well on his way to becoming an Eagle Scout. The Major was pushing.

Troop meetings began at precisely 4:00 on the first and third Tuesdays of each month, except when a camping trip was in the works. The Major strongly believed that Boy Scouts belonged in the woods and should spend as much time there as possible. Each month he planned a long weekend trip, leaving as early as possible Friday after school and returning Sunday afternoon. The troop met every Thursday before a camping trip, primarily to finalize details and get last-minute instructions from the Major.

Theo lived for the camping trips. His father was not much of an outdoorsman, and scouting gave Theo the opportunity to camp, hike, fish, learn outdoor skills, and get lost in nature. His parents encouraged scouting because Theo was an only child, and as such, perhaps, needed a bit of help in the sharing department, as well as learning the virtues of teamwork, discipline, and organization.

This weekend the troop was headed to Lake Marlo, their favorite destination. It was a large, man-made lake surrounded by steep hills, two hours away from Strattenburg. The Major was always in search of new camping areas and the troop moved around, but Lake Marlo felt like home. On the Thursday before they were scheduled to leave, Major Ludwig called the troop to order, went through the agenda, then met with his patrol leaders. Troop 1440 currently had five patrols—Panther, Rattlesnake, Ranger, Warthog, and Falcon—and each patrol had seven or eight boys. Theo was the leader of the Falcon Patrol, and it was his responsibility to check the tents, equipment, and gear, and primarily to make sure there was enough food for the weekend. He assigned chores—cooking, cleaning, campfire control, latrine maintenance, firewood, and a dozen others.

The Major reviewed the menus and work assignments and discussed the events planned for the weekend. Precamping meetings were far more exciting than the others, and the boys were ready to go. They were rowdier than usual and had some difficulty following the Major's orders. At 5:30 p.m., he adjourned the meeting and told them to clear out.

Because the Major expected perfect attendance, Theo had never missed a meeting. Neither had a kid named Hardie Quinn, a friend from school who was in another eighth-grade section. After the meeting, Hardie cornered Theo outside where a bunch of bikes were parked at a rack.

"Say, Theo," Hardie said quietly as he looked around to make sure no one else was listening. "You got a minute?"

"Sure," Theo said. "What's up?"

"You know the law pretty well, don't you?"

"Some of it, sure. My parents are lawyers and they let me hang around the office. I guess I sort of pick up some of the law."

"That's what I've heard." Hardie glanced around again as if he had a secret that might be embarrassing. This happened to Theo all the time. A friend at school or a friend of a friend would approach Theo and kick the dirt while finding the right words to describe some legal problem that Theo might be able to analyze and then offer some advice. And Theo was always willing to help, especially for nice kids like Hardie. According to the Major's plan, the two boys would make Eagle in about a year. Theo currently had twenty-three merit badges. Hardie had twenty-four. Theo was the leader of the Falcon Patrol. Hardie led the Panthers.

"Anyway," Hardie said, "have you heard about this bypass around the city?"

"Yep. Saw it on the news last night."

"Well, my grandparents got a notice in the mail yesterday that the state plans to take our farm out by Red Creek so they can run the bypass through it. This is a one-hundred-acre farm that's been in my family since the 1860s, when one of my great-great-grandfathers bought the land. Now the state says it's taking it away to build a bypass."

"Happens all the time," Theo said. "It's called the right of eminent domain."

"The what?"

Two other Scouts walked close to get their bikes. Hardie

was suddenly silent. A few seconds later, Theo said, "Is that your bike?"

"Yep."

"Good. Let's go to my office, where we can talk."

For ten minutes the boys sped through the quiet and shady streets of Strattenburg until they rolled into the gravel parking lot behind the Boone & Boone building. They entered a small rear door and stepped into Theo's office. Judge was sleeping under the desk and came to life as soon as he saw the boys. Theo had to pause and properly rub his head. "This is Judge," he said, and Hardie began rubbing too.

"Wait here," he said, and Hardie took a seat. Since it was almost 6:00 p.m., the offices were quiet. Vince the paralegal and Dorothy the real estate secretary were gone, as was Elsa at the front desk. Mrs. Boone was in her office with the door closed, a clear sign that she was meeting with a client. Mr. Boone's SUV was not in the parking lot, so he was probably not around.

Theo walked into his favorite spot, the large conference room with walls lined with thick books and a long shiny mahogany table down the middle, with a dozen leather chairs around it. The conference room was used for all sorts of important meetings, and it also doubled as the firm's library. Theo knew that many of the imposing legal books on the shelves had not been touched in years, but they were still impressive. He fetched Hardie, and they fell into the leather chairs with Judge not far away.

Hardie gawked at the walls and the long table and said, "Wow, Theo, this is pretty cool."

"This is where I like to work when the lawyers are gone."

"And your parents don't mind?" Hardie asked with some uneasiness.

"Not at all. Relax. It's just a law office."

"That's easy for you to say, Theo, but I've never been in a law office before. My dad is a minister. And his father was a minister."

Theo had met Reverend Charles Quinn at a Scout function and thought he was pretty cool. "Relax, Hardie. You may be in a real law office, but I'm not a real lawyer, so I can't charge anything."

"That's good to hear. I wasn't planning on hiring anybody. I'm just looking for information. I'm sure my parents will talk to a lawyer, and pretty soon. It's just that we're scared right now."

"Here's the deal," Theo said, getting down to business. "Eminent domain is an old legal idea that's been on the books forever. It means the state has the right to take land when it can prove that it needs the land. The state has to pay a fair price to the landowners, but the landowners can't stop the state from taking their land."

"That's outrageous. Who thought up that law?"

"Somebody in England, a long time ago. It's actually not such a bad law, because if the state can't take land when it needs to, then nothing would ever be built. Think about it. Highways, bridges, dams, parks, lakes—if one or two landowners said no, then none of these projects could go forward."

"You don't understand, Theo. My grandparents are still on this farm. They live in this great old white-frame house where we all gather for the holidays. I've spent the night there with my cousins a thousand times. We've built tree houses, zip lines, forts, bike jumps, everything you can think of. There is a long front yard where we play tackle football, baseball, Frisbee, golf, soccer, lacrosse, you name it. There are two ponds stocked with more fish than we can ever catch, and we fish there at least once a month. We've even ice fished on the front pond in the winter. We play hockey on the pond when it's cold enough. Near the house is a small barn where my grandfather keeps two ponies, Belle and Daisy, and a horse named Captain. I've been riding these guys since I could walk."

Hardie was leaning forward on his elbows, gesturing wildly with his hands. His voice was rising and shaking, and for a moment Theo thought Hardie might get choked up and start crying. He went on, "There's a place we call the Campsite. It's on the banks of Red Creek, in a bend in the river, and every cousin in my family, boys and girls, gets to camp out there on his or her fifth birthday. It's a family ritual. My dad and my uncles set up camp and all of the older cousins show up, and for two nights we have this big family birthday party. We cook over a wood grill. We tell stories around a campfire, and my uncle Jack can tell ghost stories that will scare you so bad you can't breathe. My uncle Henry knows every star in the sky, and we'll lie on our backs for hours looking at the constellations. My first merit badge was Astronomy because I've known that stuff all my life."

Hardie paused to catch his breath, then, slowly, he wiped a tear. "I'm sorry, Theo."

"It's okay, Hardie. I understand."

Hardie bit his lip, then continued: "My father and grandfather wanted us to appreciate nature and to respect the land. They took us hunting and fishing, still do. I killed my first deer when I was eight years old, then I watched my father clean it and save the meat. He made venison sausage and took it to the homeless shelter. We've never killed animals just for the sake of sport. We fish the ponds and Red Creek for bass, bream, and crappie, and I could clean and grill them in a skillet over a fire when I was ten years old. This is our land, Theo. No one has the right to take it."

Yes they do, Theo thought, but let it pass.

"Along the front drive there is a grove of sugar maples, and in the middle of it is a cemetery, a little square with a white picket fence around it. That's where all the Quinns are buried. Dozens of small tombstones, all lined up in neat rows. My great-grandparents, side by side, and next to their parents. Aunts and uncles. Edward Quinn, who died in the Second World War. Bob and Holly Quinn, great-aunt and uncle, killed in a car wreck in 1985, long before we were born. You can walk through the cemetery and relive the history of my family. Every July the Fourth we have a big cookout on the farm, and just before dinner we all walk down to the cemetery to place flowers on the graves and pay our respects. My dad has a cousin, Daniel Quinn, who's retired, and his job is to cut the grass and maintain the cemetery. What happens to the graves, Theo, to the cemetery? Surely the state can't take that part of the property. That's not right."

Theo squirmed a bit and said, "I may have to do some research, Hardie, and I'll probably talk to my dad because he's a real estate lawyer and knows a lot about eminent domain, but I don't think there is a good answer, or at least the answer you want to hear. If the state takes the property, then it owns it in every way. They'll send in the bulldozers and flatten everything."

"What about the graves, Theo?"

"I'll have to ask my dad."

Hardie sat still for a long time and gazed at the table, his thoughts far away. Finally, he said, "The house goes back a hundred and fifty years. My father has two sisters and two brothers, and since he's the oldest he gets the house when my grandparents are gone. Since I'm also the oldest, I'm supposed to get the house one day. It's the family tradition and it's worked well for a long time. It's a great old house and getting to live there is an honor, but you also have to take care of the farm. And that's a lot of work. What happens to the house, Theo?"

Theo was getting tired of tough questions he couldn't really answer. "I guess I'll have to check with my dad," he said, though he suspected he knew the truth. But Hardie was upset and Theo did not want to make things worse. After the state takes the land, the state can do whatever it pleases.

Hardie continued: "My parents were discussing this bypass last night over dinner."

"Mine too."

"It's being pushed by some trucking companies north and south of Strattenburg. They hate coming through town on Battle Street because they get clogged up in traffic. They think a bypass around town will make it easier to haul freight and do all sorts of wonderful things for their business. They give money to the politicians, including the governor, and so the politicians pull the right strings, and here we are with the state taking away our farm."

"I think my mother would agree with that. Not so sure about my dad."

"And there are also these local business guys who think they can make a buck off the bypass. Think about it. Two hundred million dollars is about to be spent right here in Strattenburg, and so a lot of folks are jumping on board."

"Like who?"

"Like construction companies, bridge builders, equipment salesmen, companies that sell materials. My dad says these guys will go nuts in support of the project. The economy is down, business is slow, and now suddenly there is this huge project. My dad says it's just a typical government pork scam. The politicians go for the votes while the businessmen scramble to make a buck. Meanwhile the taxpayers get stuck with the bill for another bad project."

"What's pork?" Theo asked.

"According to my dad, pork is when government money is given to politicians who use it to build projects in order to get votes in order to stay in office. Sometimes the projects are good, but often they aren't really needed. Pork is a bad word now in politics, but the politicians are still chasing the pork, according to my dad."

"I think my mom would agree with your dad."

"What should we do, Theo?"

"Hire a real lawyer. Eminent domain cases are tried in court before a judge who makes the decision as to how much money the property is worth. You gotta have a lawyer."

"Do you think your mother would take the case?"

"No. She just does divorces."

"What about your father?"

"He doesn't go to court."

"Can you talk to your parents and get the name of a good lawyer?"

"Sure. I'm happy to do that."

Hardie slowly got to his feet, and said, "Thanks, Theo."

"I really didn't do anything."

"You listened, and that's worth a lot."

As they left the conference room, Theo turned off the lights. Judge followed them back to Theo's office, then outside.

Chapter 6

For the second morning in a row, the Friday edition of the *Strattenburg Gazette* ran a front-page story about the Red Creek Bypass. Theo read it with great interest at the kitchen table as he and Judge ate Cheerios and prepared for another day, although it was far from just another day because he was going camping. The only bad thing about a camping trip was that dogs were not allowed. Theo and a few of the other Scouts had once asked the Major if they could bring their dogs, and they got a flat "No." The Major said his job was difficult enough keeping up with fifty city kids off in the woods. The last thing he needed was a pack of dogs running wild.

Though he didn't argue, Theo thought this was a bit

unfair. Judge was a very disciplined dog who came when he was told to come, sat when he was told to sit, rolled over when he was told to roll over, and never ran off. He stayed close to Theo at all times when they were away from home. Judge would love to camp out with the boys, and sit around a campfire, and sleep with Theo in a pup tent, and hike and swim. But when the Major said no, he meant it.

Mr. Boone was already gone; he enjoyed an early piece of wheat toast with his coffee club at a downtown diner. Mrs. Boone did not eat breakfast. Instead she usually sat in the den in her bathrobe and read the newspaper in silence. For a woman who talked all day long, she enjoyed the quietness of the early morning. Occasionally, though, like today, she sat at the kitchen table with Theo and they read the newspaper together. He was leaving for the weekend, and she wanted to be close.

According to the *Gazette*, the announcement by the governor had set off a storm of bickering by various groups in town. The tree huggers, led by the Sierra Club, the Stratten Environmental Council, and a bunch of other groups, were screaming noisy objections and threatening lawsuits. The pro-business crowd was praising the governor and the bypass and howling about how bad traffic was on Battle Street and how much this was hurting the city. A good-government group chimed in with a protest that the project was too wasteful and unnecessary. Several landowners were angry that the state planned to take their property. Hardie Quinn's family was not mentioned.

In other parts of the state, the governor was being congratulated for pushing the project. In Lowensburg, an hour south, the mayor said the absence of a bypass around Strattenburg had choked off important "avenues of commerce" and harmed the economy of his city. In Carlsburg, an hour to the north, a state senator said two factories had closed in recent years because truck traffic was so slow around Strattenburg.

The war of words raged on. As he read, Theo learned that the final decision on whether or not to build the bypass would be made by the County Commission, a board with five elected members from the five districts in the county. Two commissioners were on record favoring the bypass. Two were undecided. The fifth one could not be found at the moment.

On page two, there was a large map of Stratten County, with the city square in the middle of it. Highway 75 was a major four-lane road that ran the entire length of the state and was heavily traveled. When it got to the northern part of Strattenburg it became known as Battle Street, and that's where the problems started. To keep the old section of town from becoming too congested, city and county planners had shoved virtually all development out of the city limits and into the county. For almost thirty years, shopping centers, fast-food joints, car washes, motels, bank branches, big grocery stores, service stations, and the like had been crammed together along both sides of Battle Street, which had gone from two lanes to four to six and now to eight. There was a lot of traffic, but it moved reasonably well. The strategy had worked because the charm and character of the old sections of Strattenburg had been preserved. It was not unusual to hear people complain about the mess out on Battle Street, but in all fairness, that five-mile section of Highway 75 kept the traffic off Main Street.

The bypass would begin just north of the city limits and make a wide semicircle away from the congestion and into the rural areas. It would pass very close to Jackson Elementary School, and it would plow through a brand-new soccer complex adjacent to the school. It would destroy St. Andrew's Lutheran, a small church that dated back over two hundred years. It would require the taking, by eminent domain, of fifty homes and a dozen farms (including the Quinns'). It would reduce the values of another four hundred homes. It would wipe out the Red Creek Trail, a popular fifteen-mile hike-and-bike pathway through the hills around Strattenburg. And it would cross Red Creek in two places.

According to those in favor of the bypass, it would relieve the congestion on Battle Street by taking between twenty and twenty-five thousand vehicles a day off that street.

What a mess, thought Theo as he finished his Cheerios. However, on this Friday the arguments over the bypass belonged to someone else. Theo was going camping and little else mattered.

"What's the plan?" his mother asked as he rinsed both bowls and placed them in the sink.

"School's out at three thirty, and I'll hustle home to get my stuff. Everything's packed—clothes, sleeping bag, toothbrush, etcetera. I'll meet you here at four and you take me to the VFW."

"Sounds like a plan. Go brush your teeth." She said this every morning.

Theo ran upstairs to his bathroom, ran water in the sink, but did not brush his teeth, grabbed his backpack and returned to the kitchen.

"Do you have lunch money?" she asked, the same question five mornings a week.

"Always."

"And your homework is complete?"

"It's perfect, Mom." Theo was halfway out the door.

"Be careful, Theo, and remember to smile."

"I'm smiling, Mom."

"Love you, Teddy."

"Love you back," he said, and closed the door behind him. Judge followed him to the edge of the garage, where Theo scratched the dog's head, said good-bye, hopped on his bike, and took off. He, Theo, was not actually smiling. He had the thickest braces in the eighth grade and was dying to get rid of them. Maybe next month, his orthodontist kept saying. He mumbled the word, "Teddy," and was thankful none of his friends ever heard it. It was a baby name only his mother kept using. Even Mr. Boone had moved on to "Theo," or, occasionally when he was lecturing, "Theodore." As Theo sped away on his bike, he almost shuddered thinking about the abuse he would take if his friends every caught on to the "Teddy" business. Thirteen-year-old boys were pretty brutal when it came to nicknames, and so far Theo had avoided getting tagged with a bad one. Fred Jasper was fair-skinned with freckles and had been called Freck for so long the name was now permanent. Freck's best friend, Brandon Taylor, had dissected a bullfrog with a steak knife when he was only ten years old, and had since been known simply as Frog. Freck and Frog; you saw them together everywhere. Poor Scott Butts had an unfortunate last name that gave rise to an amazing variety of colorful, and often tasteless, nicknames and jokes. Indeed, almost every boy in the eighth grade was known by something other than his real name.

Theo had asked his mother to stop calling him Teddy, partly out of fear that someone else might hear it. She always just smiled, as if it was their private little matter. She had brought him into this world, and loved him like no other, and if Teddy was the first name she called him, then she would probably use it forever. But, she would keep it between them. Theo certainly hoped so.

Theo waved and smiled at Mr. Nunnery, a nice old man who was able to sit on his porch for hours without moving. The air was clear and cool and the weather forecast for the weekend was perfect; no rain in sight. Last month the troop camped near some Indian burial mounds in a state park and it rained for three straight days. Fun, still, but when the campsite is nothing but mud and the campfires are too soaked to burn and the food is soggy and ruined and no one has a dry stitch of clothing, well, it's time to go home.

The bus had once been painted the standard yellow and had hauled kids to and from school. It was now painted a dark green, with white trim, with BOY SCOUT TROOP 1440—OLD BLUFF

COUNCIL—STRATTENBURG in bold letters and numbers down both sides. On board were thirty-eight Scouts, all in perfect uniforms, all terribly excited to be leaving home and leaving town. Behind the wheel was Major Ludwig, the unquestioned leader of this gang, and when he called the roll and closed the door, a loud cheer echoed through the bus. It was almost 4:30 p.m. on Friday, and Lake Marlo was two hours away. The back benches were stuffed with a small mountain of camping gear, all neatly arranged under the Major's supervision. Seated behind him were three adults, fathers of various Scouts drafted as volunteers for the weekend. They would be known as the Old Goats Patrol. They sipped coffee from paper cups and laughed among themselves. It was obvious they were as excited as the boys. The bus weaved through the back streets of Strattenburg, then headed west out of town. As the traffic thinned and the miles clicked along, the excitement waned and several Scouts nodded off. Others played video games. One or two read a book. Theo was gazing out a window, a cool breeze in his face, when Hardie Quinn swapped seats and fell in beside him.

In a low voice, Hardie said, "We met at the farm last night, the whole family. Everyone's really upset by this, Theo."

Also in a low voice, Theo replied, "Has anyone talked to a lawyer?"

"Yes. My dad met with one yesterday for a long time, and the guy said the same thing. If the state wants to take our land, then it can do so. Of course, it has to pay us, but with eminent domain the state can do whatever it wants."

Theo shook his head. Hardie went on, "My poor grandparents are so upset by this. They've been married for fifty years and they've lived in only one place—the farm. If they have to leave, it'll just kill them. Both of them were crying last night. It was just awful. They don't care about the money, and they don't want the state to write them a check. They want to keep their property. It's more than just land, Theo, you know?"

Theo was listening as if he knew precisely. Hardie said, "We gotta figure out a way to fight this thing, Theo."

Theo wasn't sure how he had been drafted so quickly into the fight. "What do you mean?"

"According to my dad, it's a simple matter of politics. There are five members on the County Commission, and they have to approve the bypass. Those of us who are opposed to it have to get organized and convince the commissioners it's a bad idea. My dad and my uncles are trying to organize things as quickly as possible. They think it might be a good idea for our Scout troop to get involved."

"Why?"

"Because, Theo, this bypass could do some real damage to the environment. All of the city's drinking water comes from the Red Creek, and no one knows how much the bypass will affect it. Plus there will be all this truck traffic zooming by Jackson Elementary School. Think of the noise and exhaust fumes. It could be terrible. What if we talk to the Major about making this a project for the whole troop?"

"I'm not sure the Major will want to get involved in local politics."

Hardie thought about this for a moment, and said, "I think we should talk to him this weekend. Find a quiet moment, and just run it by him. It can't hurt anything."

"Let me think about it," Theo said. He was a little irritated Hardie would bring up such an unpleasant issue at a time of great excitement, but he gave him a break. Theo tried to imagine how he would feel if the government wanted to bulldoze the Boone home and the rest of the neighborhood to build a parkway. Of course he would be upset.

Chapter 7

The first view of Lake Marlo was always exciting, and everyone on the bus was anticipating it. The highway peeked over a steep hill, and suddenly, spread below it, were the beautiful blue waters that stretched a mile wide and seemed to run forever to their source. The lake was surrounded by rolling hills, and a long earthen dam ran half a mile to the east and kept the water contained. Because it was a state park, there had been no development along the shores—no houses, condos, marinas, no clutter. The lake was lined with narrow beaches, rocky points, and secluded bays. It was the perfect place for a bunch of Boy Scouts to get lost in the great outdoors over a long weekend.

There were dozens of campsites around the lake, and

of all varieties. The choices ran from the fancier places with slabs and sewers and electrical hookups for recreational vehicles all the way down to the primitive sites tucked away on far sides of the lake. With Major Ludwig at the wheel, the Troop 1440 bus always headed to the same spot, a site known as Enid Point, far away from the dam and the more civilized areas.

Theo had earned his Camping merit badge months earlier. A requirement was to keep a camping diary, which he had checked the night before. In his two years as a Boy Scout, he had spent twenty-one nights at Lake Marlo, either under the stars in perfect weather or in a pup tent when things were damp and cold. The previous summer, the troop had camped at Enid Point for seven consecutive nights. Various fathers, including Mr. Boone, had hauled in food and supplies. It had been a magical week, and Theo had been terribly saddened when the adventure was over.

He still dreamed of it often. During a dreary day at school, he would gaze through the windows, see the hills in the distance, and remember those wonderful carefree hours when he and the other Scouts roamed around the lake hiking, backpacking, and studying nature. They spent hours on the water, working on merit badges for Swimming, Rowing, and Lifeguarding. The Major held classes on first aid, cooking, and at night, astronomy. The days were lazy, but the Major was always pushing the boys to learn and achieve more. The First Class Scouts were pushed to achieve the rank of Star, then Life, then Eagle. There were currently 120 merit badges in the book. "You shouldn't stop until you have at least half of them," the Major was fond of saying. Sixty merit badges? It seemed impossible. Truman, a fifteen-year-old Eagle who had led the Warthog Patrol for three years and was the finest Scout in the troop, had earned forty-seven merit badges. His sash was heavily decorated and the envy of every kid in the troop. But the Major gently challenged him to do more.

Theo had already decided that in addition to being either a lawyer or a judge, he would definitely be a scoutmaster. He knew the job paid nothing, but if the Major could do it and do it so well, then he could certainly try.

The bus bounced along a gravel road and worked its way slowly up and down hills covered in thick trees and undergrowth. As they retreated from civilization, it usually took thirty minutes from the first sighting of the lake to their arrival at Enid Point. The gravel turned into dirt, and Theo could not help but remember a camping adventure here when heavy rains washed out the road and the troop was stranded for an extra day. That was the same trip when most of the pup tents began sliding downhill in the mud, and the boys had to scurry to the bus before they nearly froze. At the time it was a nightmare, but now the story seemed funny and was retold often.

Luckily, Enid Point was deserted; there were no other campers. The troop had reserved a large section, but other campers usually complicated matters. The Major huddled with the five patrol leaders and laid out the campsite. The tents and supplies were quickly unloaded as the thirty-eight Scouts hustled about. It would be dark in an hour, and as usual the patrol leaders wanted the tents up and organized by dark with dinner on the grill. Around a central fireplace, the five patrols laid out their tents in neat rows, like spokes on a wheel. Each two-man pup tent was identical to the others and pitched exactly four feet away from the next. The Major believed in strict organization and expected the campsite to be as perfect as possible.

Theo and the other leaders went through their duty rosters and assigned tasks. Friday's dinner was always a quick one, and by dark the boys were bunched around the campfire, eating hot dogs and marshmallows roasted over open flames. Mr. Bennett, of the Old Goats Patrol, smoked a pipe, and the fragrant smell wafted over the campsite. Mr. Hogan, Al's father, began telling ghost stories and proved quite talented. By the third one—a detailed account of a headless ax murderer last seen somewhere around Lake

Marlo—the Scouts were huddling even closer together. It was a troop ritual that the fathers were expected to handle the tall tales that naturally came with campfires, and, of course, the goal was to terrify the boys as much as possible.

A favorite nighttime hike was along a rocky path that bordered the shore of the lake. After dinner and ghost stories, flashlights were unpacked and the Major led the troop for a long, casual walk. They stopped on a sandy point with waves lapping the shore and looked above. There was a half moon, and because of clouds, almost no stars. The Major said they would try again on Saturday night. At ten, they were back in camp and preparing for the night.

Sleep was always difficult the first night. There was too much excitement at being in the woods, away from home, tucked into a warm sleeping bag in a small tent, with the sounds of crickets chirping and frogs croaking and deer snorting. Theo and Woody talked and listened to the murmurings from the other tents. They could hear the men, the Old Goats, talking and laughing by the campfire. Every half hour or so, the Major would patrol the site and tell the boys to quiet down and get some sleep. Eventually they did.

Theo awoke early and eased out of his sleeping bag. He put on his hiking boots and managed to crawl out of the pup tent without waking Woody, who appeared to be dead to the world. The sun was barely up, the air was crisp and cool, and the men were drinking coffee over a roaring fire in the center of the campsite. The Major had a pot of hot cocoa on a grill, and he poured Theo a cup. Why did it always taste so much better outdoors? Other Scouts staggered over, all wiping sleep from their eyes and unaware of how wild their tent hair really looked. They were boys—who cared? Their mothers and sisters were miles away. Looks and hygiene were not important, not on a camping trip. They had no plans to bathe or brush their teeth until they got home, though the Major would remind them of these necessities.

As the troop slowly came to life, there was more and more talk of breakfast. Before long the smell of bacon sizzling over an open fire filled the air. For the Falcon Patrol, Theo, who had already earned his Cooking merit badge, was helping Phillip work on his. Phillip was in charge of preparing breakfast for the eight Falcons both Saturday and Sunday, and had planned the menu in detail. For Saturday, it was scrambled eggs, link sausage, and jam on wheat bread grilled in a skillet. Phillip cooked over a low-impact fire as Theo supervised and the rest of the patrol scoured the area for firewood. The Major stopped by for a friendly reminder about the importance of campsite sanitation.

After breakfast and cleanup, the troop divided into small groups. Truman, an Eagle Scout, left on a twenty-mile hike with five others, all pursuing their Hiking merit badge. Gavin, a sixteen-year-old Eagle and the oldest guy there, left with three others in two canoes for a trip across Lake Marlo and back, a voyage that was expected to take eight hours. Other groups worked on the basics of Camping, First Aid, Nature, and Fishing.

Hardie had explained to the Major that he and Theo needed a short, private conversation with him. And during a lull in the activities, the three managed to ease away from the campsite. They hiked for ten minutes, climbed a small hill, and found a secluded spot on a rocky ledge with a great view of the lake. Hardie wasted no time. He launched into a history of his family's farm and described with great feeling how much it meant to him. He explained how the bypass would destroy not only the farm, but a lot of his family's history. His grandparents would be forced to move. He argued that Boy Scouts had the duty to protect nature and the outdoors, and the entire scouting handbook was filled with notions of conservation and protection of the environment. He wanted the entire troop, indeed all three of the different Scout troops in Strattenburg, to get organized and fight the bypass.

Theo just listened and nodded when needed. He could tell that Hardie's sincere plea was not being well received by the Major. When Hardie finished, the Major said, "I understand how you feel, but this is not a project for us. Based on what I've read and heard, this is something the politicians are fighting over. The governor wants the bypass. Some state senators north and south of Strattenburg want the bypass. Our local leaders are not sure, but they will be forced to make the decision."

"But it's not right and it's not fair," Hardie insisted. "How can the state take your property for a bad project?"

The Major smiled and pointed. "Look at this beautiful lake, Hardie. It was not created by nature. No sir." He pointed to another spot, sort of in the center of the lake. "Out there in the middle, it's about two hundred feet deep. There used to be a town there, a very small town called Coldwater. The Enid River ran through the center of the town, and about every five years the river would rise and rise and eventually flood, and not just the town of Coldwater. It was a wild river with a history of chaos. It would flood for miles up and down this valley. The farmers and landowners lost their crops, homes, and businesses, and they complained for decades about the flooding. Finally, about sixty years ago, the state decided to build a dam, tame the river, and stop the flooding. They created this lake. Herbert Marlo was the governor back then." He pointed to the dam, far in the distance and barely visible. "But guess what. Many of the people who lived around here did not want to give up their land. In spite of the flooding, in spite of everything, they fought the project. They hired lawyers and went to court and did everything possible to stop the dam. It took years. Have you heard the term 'eminent domain'?"

"Theo explained it to me," Hardie replied.

"Without the right of eminent domain, the state could not have built this lake. One landowner could have blocked the entire project, and flooding would have continued. Without eminent domain, there would be no dams, lakes, highways, state parks, canals, ports, lots of things, Hardie. It's not pleasant when you're on the bad end of eminent domain, but it's important for society as a whole."

"But this project was necessary. The bypass is not."

"There are those who think it is. It's shaping up to a nasty fight, and the Boy Scouts have no business in the middle of it. If you think it's wrong, then you should fight as hard as possible. Get involved. According to the newspaper, there are several groups already lined up to oppose the bypass. Use your energy there, but leave the troop out of it."

Theo was not surprised at the Major's position. The bypass smacked of politics, and it was no place for scouting. They hiked back to the campsite, where a long swim was being organized.

Chapter 8

After lunch, the Falcon Patrol left camp and headed for the peak of Mount Thatch, a leisurely five-mile hike that would consume most of the afternoon. Mount Thatch was nothing close to a real mountain, but more of a tall hill with some big rocks on the top. It was thick with woods and trails and adventures, and had the reputation of being well stocked with copperhead snakes. Neither Theo nor any other member of the Falcon Patrol had ever seen a copperhead, or a rattler, or any other poisonous snake for that matter, but deep in the woods there was always the chance of a sighting. Four months earlier, Al Hogan of the Warthog Patrol had spotted a copperhead near the peak of Mount Thatch, and this had thrilled the troop like nothing else. In the frenzy of the moment, Al had snapped a photo with his cell phone, posted it on Facebook, and half the kids in Strattenburg had seen the snake. When sighted, it was barely two feet long and lounging peacefully in the sun. Twenty-four hours later, though, it was being described, by Al, as "massive and very aggressive." He was lucky to have survived the encounter.

When the Falcon Patrol marched out of camp, all eight Scouts had backpacks with water, snacks, and first-aid kits. The enemy was out there, waiting, and the Scouts were prepared. The Major warned them to be careful and instructed them to return at precisely 4:00 p.m. He kept a walkie-talkie clipped to his belt and wanted updates on the hour.

But the snakes were either hiding or too frightened to attack the Falcons, and the hike proceeded with no drama. At the peak, Theo and his gang sat on rocks and ate cheese crackers and looked at the gorgeous lake below them. Theo, the wise, old historian, told the story of the small town of Coldwater and the floods and how it was still out there, two hundred feet below, an entire town wiped out. Woody called him a liar. They argued and bickered and finally bet one dollar. Theo couldn't wait to get back to camp and have the Major verify the story.

On the descent, with Theo in the lead and some of the others straggling behind, the lazy afternoon changed quickly when Percy yelled, "A copperhead!"

Every Boy Scout patrol has at least one kid who is always screwing up. The kid who forgets to pack his socks and underwear; the kid who knocks over the watercooler; the kid who forgets his flashlight and toilet paper; the kid who gets scared in the middle of the night; the kid who gets sick and vomits too close to the tents; the kid who pees too close to the tents; the kid who burns the pancakes; the kid who leaves dirty dishes; the kid who lets the campfire go out; the kid who'll always be a Tenderfoot because he's not smart enough to advance; the kid who can be dared into doing anything; and the kid who'll do anything in an attempt to prove he's either cool or brave.

And, the kid who thinks a copperhead is something to play with.

In the Falcon Patrol that kid was Percy.

On a rocky ledge near a cliff, there was indeed a copperhead, a long, thick one, frozen for the moment and glaring at the humans as they gawked at him. The eight Scouts formed a nervous semicircle and stared in disbelief at the deadly creature, which, before now, existed only in the brightly colored pages of nature books. It looked much more dangerous in real life. Aside from the danger, though, the snake's color and markings were striking. It was a very bright copper, a shiny color that seemed to glow in the sun.

It was twelve feet away, a safe distance, and it showed no sign of attacking. The boys showed no sign of advancing upon it, at least for the moment. Theo knew the boys should back away and clear the area. He knew that as the patrol leader it was his responsibility to order them away from the danger. He knew this, but he couldn't take his eyes off the snake.

"Is it really a copperhead?" someone asked.

"Sure it is," Woody said. "Look at its color and markings, and look at its triangular-shaped head. That's where the venom is." Woody had owned several snakes, of the nonpoisonous variety, and knew more about the reptiles than anyone else, though at that moment there were several experts in the group.

"It seems big for a copperhead," someone said.

Indeed it did.

"I think it's a male," added another.

"You can't tell with snakes," Woody said. "You have to pick 'em up and look on the underside."

"Let's pick him up," Percy said.

"No way," Theo barked, and the very idea of advancing on the snake made everyone take a step back.

The standoff continued in silence for a few seconds, then the snake, perhaps sensing its own danger, slowly coiled into a defensive position. (Or was it offensive?) It lifted its head as if ready to strike, its slippery black tongue darting through the air.

"Oh boy," someone said.

"Let's back away."

Instead, Percy decided to prove either his courage or his stupidity by suddenly moving toward the snake. He had a stick, a crooked tree limb, which he thrust at the copperhead.

"Get back Percy!" Theo yelled.

"You moron!" Woody yelled.

Phillip reached to grab Percy, who took another step forward with his stick. The snake struck quickly at the stick and missed. Its quickness was startling, and even Percy paused for a split second.

What happened next would be debated for months and remembered for years. Percy would swear that Phillip, the closest kid, somehow tripped him, and he, Percy, was sent sprawling toward the snake, with bad results. Phillip would swear that he attempted to grab Percy by the shoulder and Percy, already off-balance, simply fell on his own. Since the other six Falcons were staring at the copperhead, they were not sure what propelled Percy forward. However, knowing his tendencies, they would always side with Phillip.

Percy yelled in horror as he hit the ground hard and tumbled toward the snake. He screamed when the fangs made contact. The copperhead nailed him on the fatty part of his right calf, halfway between his knee and his ankle. The strike occurred as Percy was on all fours, trying to scramble away. By then everyone was yelling this and that, and in the total panic of the moment, the copperhead slithered between two rocks and disappeared.

Percy was wearing shorts, as were all the boys, and within seconds his lower right leg had a tennis ball–sized growth on it. He was wailing and crying and twisting in horror. Woody dragged him to a patch of grass and the other Scouts, all stunned by what they had just seen, circled him.

It was a Boy Scout's dream. A real, live, genuine snakebite, on the leg of someone else. It was too cool!

"Do something Theo!" Percy yelled between sobs. "Quick! I'm dying here!"

Theo was the only member of his patrol with the First Aid merit badge, plus he was the leader. All eyes were suddenly upon him. He looked at Woody and said, "Better radio the Major." Woody, the assistant patrol leader, kept a walkie-talkie on his belt. He radioed the camp and informed the Major that there was a casualty.

"What should we do?" Woody asked.

Over the air, the Major said, "Where are you?"

"We just left the peak."

"So you're two miles away. I'm on my way. Tell Theo to treat the wound."

"Okay."

Theo had already unpacked his first-aid kit. He was nervous and when he heard "treat the wound," his stomach flipped.

Bo, a clown, said, "Those snakes always travel in pairs." And every other Scout jumped out of his skin. They looked wildly around, saw nothing, then turned their attention back to Percy.

Theo attempted to take charge. He knelt beside Percy and said, "Look, first of all, you gotta lie down and stay still, okay?"

Percy yelled again. He was kicking, writhing in pain and fear. "Do something, Theo, do something!" he screamed.

"Just lie down and keep your head up. Your head has got to stay above the snakebite, okay?"

Percy seemed to hear this and for a moment tried to relax. He reclined on his elbows. Tears were dripping off his cheeks.

Woody said, "You gotta make incisions over the fang marks, right Theo? Then suck out the venom."

Theo said, "No, that's not the way to treat a snakebite."

"Yes it is!" Woody demanded. "I saw it on YouTube."

"Me too," said Phillip. "Plus that was a big snake with a

lot of venom. If we don't get it sucked out soon, they'll have to cut the leg off."

Percy wailed again.

"Can you just shut up?" Theo snapped.

Oliver knelt down opposite Theo. He had a snakebite kit already opened and ready for business. He said, "Look, Theo, I read the instructions. It plainly says you gotta make incisions over both fang marks with this little razor here." He held up the razor, which was only an inch long but suddenly seemed huge. Oliver went on, "Says you gotta make an X over each fang mark, then insert the suction tube to extract the venom."

"Why don't you just shoot me first?" Percy said, crying again.

"That's the old-fashioned way of treating a snakebite," Theo said.

"But this is a brand-new snakebite kit."

"I don't care."

"I thought you were supposed to put a tourniquet two inches above the bite," Phillip observed, helpfully.

"Anybody else got a stupid opinion?" Theo barked.

Oliver looked at Percy and said, "Look, Percy, I think we need to suction out the venom. But it's your leg. What do you think?"

Percy said, "I think I'm a dead man with you clowns in charge." He closed his eyes, then said, "Hey, Theo, I'm getting pretty dizzy."

"Move back," Theo said. He quickly wrapped the wound with a sterile bandage and taped it into place. Percy was whimpering but had stopped the kicking and jerking. Theo said, "Here's what we're going to do. We have to get him back to the camp, then to a hospital. Let's carry him as gently as possible down the trail until we meet the Major. Be sure to keep the snakebite below his heart. Phillip, you go first and look out for snakes."

Oliver said, "I think we ought to slice it open and use the suction cup. Back in the old days they sucked out the venom with their mouths. If you had a cavity, the venom went straight to your brain and you died faster than the guy who got bit."

"Would you just shut up!" Theo snapped again.

They lifted Percy off the ground and draped his arms around the necks of Woody and Cal. Theo cradled his wounded leg and Oliver took his left one. "Easy now," Theo said. "We have to keep him still. Otherwise, the venom circulates too fast. Percy, you might feel queasy. If you need to throw up, just say something. No surprises. Okay?"

"Okay." Percy was breathing heavily and had stopped

crying. To avoid looking at his leg, he closed his eyes. The leg was getting bigger.

They shuffled down the trail with the patient getting heavier by the moment. After ten minutes, they stopped to rest. Theo said, "Talk to me, Percy. You gotta stay awake."

"I'm awake," he said with a weak voice.

"Do you feel sick?"

"Well, my leg certainly does."

"How about your stomach?"

"Not yet. Am I doing to die, Theo?"

"No. It's just a copperhead. They don't kill people, but you'll be sick as a dog."

"That was a big snake, wasn't it?"

"Yes, it was."

"Did anybody get a picture?"

The Scouts looked at each other and realized they had been too stunned by the encounter to take a photo. "I guess not," Theo said.

"Should I call my mom?" Percy asked.

"I think the Major should do that. Let's go."

They lifted him again and continued down the trail. The boys were exhausted when they saw the Major coming around a bend. He was with Mr. Hogan and Mr. Bennett. Percy was still conscious and still complaining of dizziness. They took him to a small open area near a boat ramp and laid him on a picnic table. The Major removed the sterile bandage for a look at the bite, and it was obvious he was impressed by the swelling. As they waited, Percy began clutching his stomach. Soon, he was vomiting.

The Major held him and kept a wet towel on his forehead and mouth. The more Percy vomited, the more he cried. It was a pitiful scene.

Finally, they heard the helicopter.

Chapter 9

It was a quiet dinner. Very quiet, very subdued. The Falcon Patrol kept to itself, hovered over its campfire, and ate chicken breasts grilled in a skillet and potatoes wrapped in foil and baked in the coals. When it was dark, they moved to the central campfire and joined the other patrols. All of Troop 1440 was quiet and deep in thought. The Major had phoned from the hospital where the medevac helicopter had taken him and Percy. Percy's parents had arrived and things seemed to be under control. Fortunately, the hospital had plenty of antivenom for copperhead bites, and Percy was stable and sedated.

His buddies around the fire talked softly as they roasted marshmallows and glowed in the warmth of the burning logs. They wanted to ask the tough questions, like (1) will he die? Or (2) will he lose his leg? But they showed restraint. Oddly enough, they began telling snake stories. This made no sense whatsoever because they were nervous and jumpy anyway. Every leaf that rustled in the wind might have been a rattler. Every burning log that hissed might have been some unknown viper. Every branch snapping in the distance might have been another large copperhead easing up on them from the rear. And every ten minutes or so one Scout would sneak behind another, pop him in the neck with two fingers, and yell "Snake!" This was nerve-racking humor that produced a lot of nervous laughter. Mr. Bennett eventually moved the stories away from the serpents and back to more suitable topics like zombies and vampires.

Around 9:00 p.m., headlights approached the campsite. It was the Major arriving from the hospital. He stood in front of the troop near the campfire and gave the latest update on Percy and his wound. There was a lot of swelling in the leg and Percy felt lousy in general, but he was awake and expected to be fine. After a couple of days in the hospital, he would be released and sent home. The doctor's biggest concern was the damaged skin around the bite. There was dead tissue and they expect some scarring.

After the Major ate a quick dinner, he asked the surviving members of the Falcon Patrol to join him down by the lake. They sat on logs not far from where the waves were gently splashing against the rocks of the shoreline. There was a full moon; it was a beautiful night; and there should not have been any problems.

However, Theo suspected trouble.

The Major asked Woody to go first and tell what happened. Woody gave a true and accurate account of the encounter with the copperhead. When he finished, the Major sent him back to the campsite. Cal went next with his story, then left. He was followed by Phillip, then Oliver, then the rest.

Suddenly, Theo was alone. Just him and the Major, who, at the moment, was looking at the moon's reflection across the lake. "Do you agree with everyone else, Theo?" he asked.

Without hesitation, Theo answered, "Yes sir."

The Major turned around and sat down next to Theo on the log. He cleared his throat and asked, "As a patrol leader, what are you supposed to do when your patrol confronts a dangerous animal?"

"Depends on the animal," Theo replied.

"And in this case, it was a poisonous snake."

"Then I'm supposed to immediately warn my patrol to move away from the snake and leave the site as soon as possible."

"And is that what you did, Theo?"

Theo swallowed hard and said, "No sir."

"Did you immediately recognize the snake to be a copperhead?"

"Yes sir."

"How many poisonous snakes do we have in this part of the country?"

"Three. Copperhead, coral snake, and the timber rattler."

"And you knew this through your study for the Nature merit badge?"

Theo had watched enough *Perry Mason* reruns and real-live courtroom trials to know the Major was setting him up for the kill. Slowly, he answered, "Yes sir."

There was a long, painful pause as they watched the moonlit lake and waited for the Major to speak next. Finally, he said, "So, Theo, it looks as though the Falcon Patrol, while hiking in an area well-known for copperheads, actually encountered such a snake, and a large one, and instead of immediately taking steps to avoid the snake, did just the opposite. The patrol instantly moved closer, for a closer look, and at some point Percy picked up a stick and decided to agitate the snake. You, as a patrol leader, finally had the presence of mind to order everyone back, but by then, Percy, who we all know is probably not the most reliable Scout in the troop, somehow lost his balance, fell forward, practically on top of the snake, and was bitten. Is this a fair summary, Theo?"

Theo would probably change a word or two, but it seemed like a bad time to quibble. The Major had the important points dead center.

Theo bit his lip and said, "Yes sir."

Another long pause. There was laughter in the distance from the campfire. Lucky guys.

The Major said, "Okay, Theo, pretend you're a lawyer and give me your best defense."

Finally, Theo thought to himself, and he did not waste a second. "The story you've heard is a correct version of what happened, but there were a few other factors involved. First, we were naturally on the lookout for copperheads, and most of the Falcons had snakebite kits in their backpacks. The wrong kind of kits, but let's just say we were prepared. So when we actually saw a copperhead, and one that was so big and so beautiful it was impossible not to stop for a second to admire it, that's what we did. We stopped to admire it. Don't you think that's human nature? You're in the woods, looking for adventure, looking for excitement, and, suddenly you find it in the form of a dangerous snake. You can't believe your good luck. You gotta stop for a second and stare at it. Everyone does that, or at least every Boy Scout. Sure we moved a little closer, but I did not lead my patrol into a dangerous situation. No sir. From where we were standing, the snake could not have struck us, and it was not moving toward us. We were not in danger; close, maybe, but not within striking range. The snake was stretched out on the narrow ledge, and when it slowly coiled itself up, either in defense or offense, don't know for sure because how can you ever know for sure, I told the patrol to back away. For a second, no one moved, not even me, but you could tell that we were ready to bolt. Then stupid little Percy stepped forward with a stick and decided to have some fun. As soon as I saw the stick, I yelled for him to back up, but within a split second he was falling forward. He's lucky he wasn't bitten in the neck or face."

The Major listened thoughtfully and considered every word. When Theo finished, there was another long gap in the conversation as they stared at the water. Finally, the Major said, "Leadership requires many things, Theo. Detailed planning, the ability to plan for the future, and so on, but it can also require a cool head in the heat of battle. I learned that in combat, where I often had to make life-and-death decisions in a split second. Your timing wasn't so good, Theo. You should have cleared the area immediately."

"You're blaming me for Percy's snakebite?"

"Not entirely. But under the circumstances, you failed to act properly."

"Okay, if I had yelled for everyone to get away as soon as the snake was spotted do you really think Percy would have listened to me? He never does what he's told. He doesn't listen to me. He doesn't listen to you. He doesn't listen to his parents or his teachers. He was suspended from school last month for three days for setting off a pack of firecrackers during a violin concert. For the last campout he forgot to pack a toothbrush, clean underwear, clean socks, and a flashlight. He's flunked the Tenderfoot exam twice. He's an idiot, you know that much yourself."

"Maybe that's why Percy needs scouting, Theo. He needs to learn discipline and success."

"Good luck."

The Major turned and stared at Theo. He said, "You're one of our leaders and one of our best Scouts, but today, Theo, you failed under pressure. You allowed your patrol to get too close to a dangerous animal, with a bad result. We have a Scout in a hospital with a badly swollen leg and some level of permanent scarring. It could've been worse. Theo, I have no choice but to suspend you from your leadership of the Falcon Patrol. I don't want to embarrass you so let's keep this quiet until our next meeting. Not a word, okay?"

Theo wanted to dislike the Major, but the fact was he admired him greatly, even adored him and wanted to imitate him. The Major had fought in wars, flown fighter jets, traveled the world, had two or three successful careers, and now, for fun, dedicated himself as a volunteer scoutmaster in a near full-time capacity. Theo ached at the thought that the Major believed he had failed his patrol in some way.

But the Major was a tough Marine, and Theo could try and be one as well. He swallowed hard, gritted his teeth, and said, "Yes sir."

Clouds rolled in quickly, and the night was suddenly black. Theo followed the Major back to the campsite, where things were winding down as the ghost stories and snake stories were losing some of their appeal. The campfire was extinguished, the food secured, and the Scouts drifted off to their tents. Every sleeping bag was shaken and carefully inspected for snakes. Every tent was examined by flashlights, inch by inch. The areas around the tents, the tall grass and undergrowth, rocks, and even latrines were searched, then searched again. Slowly, the Scouts entered their tents, zipped the doors, crawled into the sleeping bags, then waited for the sounds of serpents creeping toward them across the wet grass. When things were perfectly quiet and still, some bozo in the Warthog section let loose with a loud "*Hisssss*," and this seemed funny to a few.

For the first time in his scouting career, Theo just wanted to go home.

Chapter 10

The rain began before dawn, and by sunrise everything was soaked. As well-trained Scouts, they were prepared for bad weather, but the cold wind and mud took most of the fun out of camping. Usually, on Sunday morning, the Major led the troop on a short hike to some spot with a beautiful view where he conducted a chapel service. He wasn't a preacher or a minister and did not require all Scouts to attend. He was, though, a wise man with a deep faith in God and a true admiration for what He created here on Earth. Theo always enjoyed these hilltop chapel services, which he found far more meaningful than those conducted indoors in a real church. But with the rain falling, the Major decided to skip chapel, hurry up with breakfast, and break camp.

By 10:00 a.m., the old green bus was loaded and moving slowly away from Enid Point, inching uphill with its tires spinning in the mud. It eventually made it to a paved road and everyone relaxed. As it gained speed and began humming down the road, many of the Scouts closed their eyes and drifted away. During the night, most had slept on and off. When they managed to fall asleep they dreamed of monstrous vipers with sharp fangs dripping with deadly venom, and when they were awake they could practically hear the snakes out there, just beyond their tents. Now, in the safety of their bus and headed home, they were suddenly overcome with fatigue.

The weather turned even worse. Traffic was slow and they passed two serious auto accidents as they crept toward Strattenburg. The two-hour drive became four, and the Scouts grew tired of the bus. When it crossed the Yancey River and rolled into downtown, they let out a cheer. At the VFW, they unloaded their muddy gear and made plans to clean it the following afternoon.

By 3:00 p.m., Theo was home. Fresh from a long shower, he sat with Judge in the den and ate chicken noodle soup while his father read the Sunday newspaper and his mother flipped through a novel.

The Major flatly refused to allow his Scouts to take

their cell phones and laptops on camping trips. Camping was a great getaway, an outdoor adventure far from most of modern civilization, and he didn't want to ruin things by the parents getting hourly updates on everything the Scouts were doing. Nor did the Major tolerate pushy parents who made demands and wanted special treatment for their unique little boys.

So, Theo's parents had not heard the news about the great snakebite. After he finished eating, and Judge was licking the bowl, Theo told them the story.

His mother was horrified, while his father found it amusing. They didn't know Percy or his parents, and Theo did a fine job of describing what a misfit the kid really was. He went on to tell about his late-night meeting with the Major, and ended it all with the news that he was being suspended for two months as the leader of the Falcon Patrol.

"That's absurd," his mother said. His father seemed to agree. For half an hour they discussed, and often debated, the actions taken by Theo and the decision made by the Major. At one point, Theo announced, "I'm thinking about quitting scouting."

Both parents went silent.

Theo continued: "The Major thinks a Scout patrol is just like a Marine unit where everyone follows orders perfectly. Doesn't work that way. We're not that disciplined. I can't bark orders and boss people around. Nothing I could've said or done would've kept Percy away from that snake. I think the punishment is too harsh and unfair."

"I agree," said his mother.

"Maybe so," said his father, "but quitting seems to be an overreaction. You love scouting, Theo. You're on the fast track to becoming an Eagle Scout. Seems a shame to throw it all away because of one incident."

"Your father is right, Theo. Quitting is not the answer. Life is not fair, and you can't quit every time something unfair happens to you."

"But I didn't do anything wrong," Theo protested. "The entire event happened in a matter of seconds. I couldn't have prevented it."

"So what?" his father said. "Your scoutmaster thinks otherwise. He's the leader, the boss, a man you happen to admire greatly and a man who thinks a lot of you. You can't convince me Major Ludwig would ever be unfair to you, Theo. Or to anyone else for that matter."

His mother added, "Theo, you said yourself many times that your troop is lucky to have such a great scoutmaster. This time you disagree with him. He's responsible for forty or so kids away from home during a long weekend. That's an enormous responsibility, and Major Ludwig does it every month. That's a lot of pressure on anyone. Now, a kid got hurt, and when something goes wrong the boss is ultimately responsible. Percy's parents will blame the Major, the whole troop, and probably the entire Boy Scouts of America."

"They'll probably sue," Mr. Boone managed to insert.

Mrs. Boone continued, "Think about the next time, Theo. The next time a group of Scouts is hiking through the woods and they come upon a poisonous snake. They'll remember this episode. The patrol leaders will be quick to retreat, and maybe no one will get hurt."

To which Theo responded, "Or maybe it'll be Percy again and he'll get tangled up with another snake."

Mr. Boone lifted his newspaper as if he needed to continue reading it. "Quitting is not the answer, Theo. Hang in there, get tough, double up on your merit badge work, and show the Major you can take the punishment." And with that he disappeared behind the sports section.

Mrs. Boone was a bit more sympathetic, but not much. She said, "If you quit, Theo, you will regret it for the rest of your life. You're only young once, and there's only one chance to succeed in scouting. It's been great fun until now, very rewarding, so don't let one bad episode ruin everything. Your father and I will be sorely disappointed if you drop out."

Theo was often amazed at how other kids' parents were so quick to butt in and cause trouble. They sent e-mails to teachers at school complaining about this and that. They harassed coaches after practices and even after games if so-and-so didn't play enough. They marched into Mrs. Gladwell's office unannounced and defended their kids when their kids were clearly wrong. They threatened to sue if so-and-so got cut from the team, or excluded from the school play, or didn't make the cheerleading squad.

At the moment, though, he sort of wished his own parents could show a little more support. Now they were both reading. Judge had a full stomach and was asleep with his tongue hanging out. No one wanted to listen to Theo, so he went upstairs to kill time on his laptop.

Monday morning, and Theo was not excited about starting another week of school, and with good reason. By the time he sat at his desk in Mr. Mount's homeroom at 8:40, he had already been asked a dozen times about the great snakebite.

Percy's mother had evidently taken a photo of her poor child as he lay wounded in a hospital bed over in Knottsburg. The photo captured Percy's smiling and goofy face, but the center point was his bare, swollen leg. And it was really puffed up. Like all smart people who want to share their private lives with the world, his mother then posted the photo on Percy's Facebook page, and she, or someone, added a brief story describing how the brave Scout had gotten himself tangled up with an "eight-foot copperhead" and its "jagged" fangs.

Of course, no blame whatsoever was laid on Percy. No, sir. An "unidentified" member of the Falcon Patrol was accused of shoving and tripping the poor boy in such a manner as to make him fall directly upon the snake, who was further described as "unusually aggressive." Reading the story, one easily got the impression that Percy had been minding his own business and hardly aware that a snake was nearby.

The photo was posted Sunday night while Theo was reading a book and ignoring his laptop. By Monday morning, it looked as though he was the only kid in school who hadn't seen it. The story dominated all gossip in the hallways and homerooms, and by the time the bell rang for first period, there were rumors that poor Percy might lose a leg.

He was becoming a legend. Out of a school with 320 students, he was the only kid who'd ever been bitten by a poisonous snake. Percy Dixon was now famous, and not because he had accomplished anything.

Famous because he was a jerk, Theo thought as he seethed and bit his tongue and gritted his way through the day. Only in America.

Theo was sick of Percy and his snakebite. As soon as possible after the final bell, he hurried to the VFW. Behind the building, the Major had scattered all of the pup tents and gear and was washing down the large coolers. About half of the troop showed up for the extra work, but Theo didn't worry about the absentees. He and Phillip and Cal immediately went about the job of pitching the Falcon tents and wiping off mud with soap and water. The tents had to be cleaned and dried; if not, they would mildew in storage.

The Major kept his distance, and Theo was fine with that. The tough old Marine loved discipline and was not about to show a softer side. Theo understood this. He had decided he would not quit scouting. He would not allow one bad moment to take away something so important to him. Instead, he would follow his father's rather cold advice and dig in, tough it out, work harder, and carry his suspension like a badge of honor. As best he could, Theo would act like a Marine and give the Major a dose of his own medicine.

As he was rolling up a tent, he heard the Major's voice behind him. "Theo, where's Woody?"

Theo stood and looked up at the Major. He thought about saying: "Gee, Major, I don't know. It's not my day to keep up with him." Or: "Gee, Major, I don't know, since he's now the patrol leader, why don't you go find him yourself." But these thoughts passed quickly, as Theo knew better than to play wise guy with the boss.

Theo said, "Not sure, but I think he had something after school." Woody was one of Theo's best friends, and Theo would do nothing to get him in trouble. The truth was that Woody had no desire to be a patrol leader and was not about to clean muddy tents on a perfectly fine Monday afternoon.

The Major clenched his jaws as he always did, then said, "I'm having an Aviation merit badge meeting this Thursday at four p.m. Can you be here?"

"Thought I was suspended," Theo shot back, then wished he had said something else.

"You're suspended as a patrol leader, not from scouting," the Major said coolly.

Theo thought for a moment. How cruel was this? At a time when he planned to stiff-arm the Major as much as possible, the guy brings up the Aviation merit badge. At the moment, Theo was working on four merit badges— Aviation, World Government, Computers, and Veterinary Science—all nice subjects and all chosen by him. The other three, though, were not nearly as exciting as Aviation. The Major had promised Theo and the other five Scouts in the study group that they would visit a regional airport, see the inside of an air traffic control center, and, best of all, take a real flight in a small Cessna.

"Okay," Theo said.

"Great. See you Thursday." And with that, the Major turned around and began barking at two guys in the Warthog Patrol.

Theo was no match for the Major, and he knew it.

Chapter II

L ate Monday afternoon, Theo rode his bike four blocks from his office in the rear of Boone & Boone to the office of another Boone—his uncle Ike's. This second Boone office was not busy or thriving or well decorated. Instead, it was on the second floor of a shabby old building that housed a Greek deli on the ground floor. Theo's father and Ike were brothers, and at one time had been lawyers together. Those days were long gone. For reasons Theo would probably never understand, Ike was no longer a lawyer and he seldom spoke to Theo's father. However, Ike was still a part of the family, and for this reason Theo was expected to stop by every Monday afternoon and chat with Ike. Often, the meetings were not too pleasant, and Theo did not always look forward to them. Other times, though, Ike could be funny and when in a good mood could tell hilarious stories. Theo never knew which Ike he would encounter on Monday afternoons. Among the family secrets was the rumor that Ike drank too much, and Theo suspected that influenced whether he felt fine or miserable.

Judge was usually confined to either the home or the office, but occasionally Theo hooked a leash to his collar and allowed him to run alongside his bike as he zipped through town. For Judge, there was no greater thrill than flying down the street trying to outrun Theo and the bike. On this Monday, Judge really wanted to go, so Theo grabbed the leash.

The two of them bounded up the stairs and, with a quick and meaningless knock, burst through the door to Ike's long and cluttered office.

"Well, well," Ike said with a smile. "How is my favorite nephew?"

"Great, Ike, and you?" Theo said as he fell into a creaky wooden chair, one with papers and files stacked under it. Every piece of furniture in the room was either covered with files or trying to hide them. Theo was Ike's only nephew, and, as far as Theo could tell, about the only family member who kept in contact with him. Ike's wife had divorced him years earlier when he got into trouble, and his kids had moved far away. Ike was a lonely old man, but at the same time it was hard to feel sorry for him. He seemed to want a quiet, unusual life.

"Just another fine day," Ike said, waving an arm at the pile of papers on his desk. "Sorting out the money problems of people with no money. How are things over at Boone and Boone?"

"The same, nothing new."

"How are your grades? Straight A's?"

"Close." This always irritated Theo, this intrusion into his privacy. He did not understand why Ike thought he had the right to nose around in Theo's schoolwork. But, as Mrs. Boone always said, "He's family."

"What do you mean 'close'?" Ike asked.

"B plus in Chemistry, but I'll pull it up."

"You better pull it up," he said sternly, but Theo could tell it was all an act. Ike looked to his left, at his desktop monitor. "This just came across. Saw it ten minutes ago," he said as he peered over his reading glasses, then clicked his mouse. "According to our fearless daily newspaper, online edition, no less, a kid from your Scout troop had a rather nasty encounter with a copperhead over the weekend. Know anything about it?"

"And why is that news?" Theo said in disgust.

"Because everything is news these days, Theo. Nothing

is private. There are no secrets and there is no shame. Everybody is a celebrity. Percy Dixon?"

"That's him, and evidently his mother is trying to get all the publicity she can. I'm sure she called the newspaper. How else would a reporter hear of something so unimportant?"

"Were you there?"

"Oh yes."

"What happened?"

So Theo told the story again.

When he finished, Ike said, "What a jerk! You don't deserve a suspension for that."

"It's okay, Ike. I'm over it, and I'm tired of talking about it. Let's change the subject."

"Sure. Yankees and Twins?"

"No." Ike was a rabid Yankees fan who loved the team and its history. Theo pulled for the Twins because no one else in Strattenburg did. In all fairness to the Twins, though, Minnesota was a thousand miles away.

"I can't blame you," Ike said. He shoved his chair back and reached for a small refrigerator he kept almost hidden behind a stack of files. He pulled out a bottle of beer for himself and a can of Sprite, which he slid across the desk, knocking off a few papers along its route. "Here," he said, just in time for Theo to catch the Sprite. Ike unscrewed the top of the beer, slowly, almost painfully, lifted his feet into position and plunked them down on his desk. When he was properly kicked back and reclined, he took a sip.

Theo knew from experience that a long story was coming.

Another sip, and Ike began, "Get a load of this." This was Ike's usual opening line for a story. "The Greek family downstairs, Jimmy and Amelda Tykos, lovely people, I've known them for years and see them every day. They came to this country when they were children and have worked twenty-four/seven their entire lives to give something to their kids. Great folks. Their oldest son, Russell, owns a construction company, builds small houses and does remodeling jobs, stuff like that. Russell's about forty, married with three kids, and his first child was born with a bunch of medical problems. They spent a fortune saving the kid and now the poor child needs all sorts of special treatment. It almost broke Russell along with his parents, but they dug in, worked harder, saved even harder, and they survived."

Theo must have glanced away, because Ike snapped, "Am I boring you here, Theo?"

"I'm listening." Theo suspected he was probably the

only person in town who would tolerate Ike's long, rambling stories, but they usually led to an interesting point.

Ike took a sip of beer, looked at the ceiling, and continued: "About ten years ago, Russell and his wife bought some land outside of town, cut it up, and began selling two-acre lots. Beautiful country, hills and creeks and ponds and such. The idea was to sell large lots to people who wanted to preserve the land and trees and protect the environment. Russell and his wife designed their dream home and started building it themselves. After hours, weekends, vacations— they spent every spare moment out there, with their kids, including the little boy in a wheelchair, slowly building their home. For the big stuff, Russell used his construction crews, but if anything could be done by two people, then it was Russell and his wife. Obviously, it was a labor of love, and it took forever. Almost five years from start to finish, and they paid cash along the way. Didn't owe a dime to anyone once they finished. They had a big move-in party and invited me. I was there. It was wonderful, all their family, and friends and neighbors, all the construction guys who'd worked on the house, everybody who'd lent a helping hand. I've never seen Jimmy and Amelda so happy and proud. Beautiful home, beautiful countryside. One big happy family, celebrating the best our country has to offer. Everything was just great."

Ike's voice trailed off, and Theo knew the first chapter

of the story was finished and it was time for him, Theo, to push things along. "So what happened?" he asked.

"Well, now the house is about to be bulldozed so the state and a bunch of politicians can build a two-hundred-million-dollar bypass around Strattenburg. The bypass is totally unnecessary, but that's not important in the game of politics. Have you heard of this bypass, Theo?"

Theo was stunned. He had almost forgotten about it. The past forty-eight hours of his life had revolved around scouting, Percy, a rather large copperhead, and a lot of garbage on Facebook.

He nodded and said, "Yes, I've heard about it."

Ike yanked his feet down. He leaned forward on his elbows, his eyes glowing with anger.

"Do you understand the legal concept of eminent domain, Theo?"

"I do."

Ike nodded and smiled. "Good for you. In theory, eminent domain is to be used as a last resort. Taking away property against the wishes of the property owner is almost a criminal act, something the government is supposed to do when absolutely necessary. In this case, there is no necessity whatsoever. It's just a bunch of politicians trying to get votes by building a road to make their big donors happy."

It rarely took much for Ike to start preaching, but on

this issue he was steamed up more than usual. Theo decided to prod him along. "I'm not sure I understand," he said.

He barely got the words out before Ike was talking again. "It's like this, Theo. In Carlsburg and places north of here, there are some big trucking companies and lots of factories and the same south of here in Lowensburg. Studies have shown that a bypass might save the truckers all of a few minutes around town, but they don't care. They want a bypass at all costs! So they get in thick with their politicians, give them a bunch of money, tell them how badly they need a bypass, not for themselves, of course, but for the sacred goal of 'economic development.' That's what every politician says whenever he wants to approve something or build something or waste some more taxpayer money. More jobs, more tax revenues, more everything, all in the name of economic development. There's also more pollution, more congestion, more crowded schools, and more developers getting rich, but the politicians never mention this because they're taking money from the developers, and, in this case, the trucking companies."

Ike took a deep breath, followed by a long drink of beer. Typical Ike, never wishy-washy, never straddling the fence, never at a loss of an opinion. Theo was actually enjoying the story because Ike was so fired up.

Theo decided to throw a little gas on the fire. "Isn't the governor pushing it?"

"What an idiot! He'll support anything if the price is right. Front-page news last week showed where the trucking companies and developers have donated tons of money to the governor's campaign, so guess what? If they want a bypass, he wants a bypass. The guy is nothing but a politician who's looking to run for a higher office. Don't ever get involved in politics, Theo. It's a dirty game."

"Don't worry."

Ike relaxed and rocked back in his chair. "Fifteen years ago, Theo, if my politics had been right, I would not have been prosecuted."

And for the first time ever, Uncle Ike mentioned his past troubles. Theo wanted to pounce with a dozen questions, but he bit his tongue. One day Ike would tell him the whole story, but he would do so when he wished. Not now.

Theo thought about telling the Hardie Quinn story, but decided to let it pass. In his opinion, his story was far more interesting than Ike's, but Ike preferred talking over listening. "Are you going to help the Tykos family?" Theo asked.

"Help? In what way?"

"I don't know, Ike. There seems to be a lot of opposition.

If enough people get involved, then maybe the county commissioners will not approve the bypass."

"Don't kid yourself, Theo. Money talks, and the side with the money always wins, especially in politics."

Theo found this depressing and didn't know what to say. Ike reached for a sheet of paper, found it, and leaned forward again. "Take a look at this, Theo," he said, and Theo leaned in. It was a copy of a map with the proposed bypass highlighted in red. Using a pen, Ike tapped a spot in the center of the page and said, "There is where the bypass will cross Sweeney Road. Right now all of this is rural land, but that will change overnight when they build it."

Theo could smell the beer on Ike's breath and it wasn't pleasant. He pulled back a few inches. Ike went on, "Now, I have a source who says that a certain local developer, guy by the name of Joe Ford, a real slick operator who's also known as Fast Ford, has put down some money to buy two hundred acres right here at the intersection of Sweeney and the bypass. It was supposed to be a secret deal, but my source knows one of the former partners of the lawyer who represents the landowner. It's hush-hush." Ike left the map on the desk and reared back in his chair. "So, Theo, the buzzards are already circling, waiting for the kill. If the county approves the bypass, you'll see these thugs scoop up every inch of land alongside it, and in ten years it'll be lined with strip malls and fast-food joints and car washes. The whole western part of the county will be covered in sprawl and look like the rest of America. The developers will get richer and they'll be happy to pass along enough cash to keep the politicians happy. It's a rotten system, Theo."

Theo was even more depressed, but then he tried to convince himself that Ike was a gloomy person by nature. Ike seldom smiled and was often bitter. His family had abandoned him and he'd been disgraced when he lost his license to practice law.

Ike and his sources. He was always claiming to know something that was supposed to be a secret, and, in fact, he often did. Ike moved in the shadows around certain parts of town, places many upstanding citizens avoided. He played poker with at least two groups, and some of those guys were ex-lawyers, ex-cops, and a few ex-cons. He gambled on football and basketball games and hung around with bookies and other gamblers. Theo's father had once let it slip that Ike made more money from betting then he did from his real work.

"Well, on that happy note, I need to go," Theo said, suddenly anxious to hit the road.

"Say hi to your folks," Ike said as he locked his fingers behind his head and returned his feet to the top of his desk.

"See ya, Ike," Theo said as he and Judge headed for the door.

"And I want an A in Chemistry."

"Sure. You and everybody else."

ercy Dixon made a triumphant return to school Tuesday morning. Theo knew something was up when he wheeled to a stop at his usual bike rack and saw a television van parked in front of the school. Sure enough, a few moments later a station wagon appeared. Percy's mother parked it, pulled out a wheelchair, lifted her son into it, and began their little parade into the building. Percy's leg was elevated and wrapped in layers of white gauze. His teachers and friends were waiting at the front door, and his mother rolled him into the school like a hero returning from war. A reporter and a cameraman followed along, capturing this "breaking news" so the peaceful town of Strattenburg would know the latest.

Theo watched from a distance, uncertain who was enjoying the spotlight more, Percy or his mother. Percy attacked the snake, and Theo got suspended. It still didn't seem fair.

Throughout the day, Theo was continually distracted by the sight of Percy rolling down the hall, or sitting in the cafeteria, or getting pushed around the playground, always with a group of admirers huddled around him as he told and retold the story of his near-deadly encounter with the copperhead, a snake that somehow was growing larger and meaner with each passing hour.

Some of the kids viewed Theo as the one who was responsible for the disaster; most, however, knew the truth. Percy had few believers, but that didn't stop him from savoring the attention.

Theo just suffered through the day, trying to ignore the sideshow. At times, he wished the snake had nailed Percy right between the eyes.

After the final bell, Theo hustled to Boone & Boone, checked on Judge, and disappeared into his office to crank out his homework. Both of his parents were in their offices behind locked doors, meeting with clients, and the entire law firm was quiet and busy. Theo finished his homework in less than an hour. It started raining, there was no place to go, and he was soon bored.

Out of curiosity, he began searching the Internet for stories about the Red Creek Bypass. There were plenty— old newspaper articles, maps, studies, angry letters to the editors. There was even a website run by a rowdy group of opponents who were collecting and posting every possible bit of information about the project. Most, of course, was not favorable, but there were a few articles from the pro-business crowd claiming the bypass was necessary.

After an hour of browsing, Theo was bored again. The rain was heavier; Judge was snoozing; his parents were still locked away in their offices. He drifted through the storage room, down the narrow hallway, and into the kitchen, where he looked around for something to eat. "Borrowing" food from another member of the firm was a sport around the offices, and Theo was often the leading culprit. Today, though, he saw nothing of interest.

Elsa was not at her desk, which was unusual. Occasionally she ran errands late in the afternoon when no more clients were expected, and Theo figured she had just stepped outside. Her desk was in the reception room, guarding the front door. When you walked into Boone & Boone you had to deal with Elsa, who ran the place like a drill sergeant. She knew everyone's schedule—the lawyers, Mr. and Mrs. Boone; Vince the paralegal; Dorothy the real estate secretary; even Theo, the kid lawyer. Somehow, Elsa kept up with all meetings, court dates, medical and dental appointments, birthdays, etcetera. She missed nothing.

Theo was curious about who was in his father's office. Woods Boone was a real estate lawyer who never went to court and rarely had clients upstairs. For at least eight hours a day, he sat at his desk, smoked his pipe, shuffled papers, drafted contracts, researched, and talked on the phone. In Theo's opinion, his father practiced a rather boring brand of law, one that he wanted no part of. No sir. Theo planned to be in the courtroom in big trials, in front of juries with crowds watching and serious drama unfolding.

Theo had watched his first trial three years ago at the age of ten. It was during the summer, he was out of school, and for four days he sat in the front row and heard every word from every witness. A young mother and father and their five-year-old son had been killed in a terrible collision with a train at a crossing. Emotions were high, and even Theo felt the pressure. The lawyers battled like gladiators, and Theo's friend Judge Henry Gantry presided over the trial with great wisdom.

From that moment, Theodore was destined for the courtroom. Occasionally, he thought of becoming a great judge like Henry Gantry, but more often his plans and dreams centered on being a fearless trial lawyer.

Elsa kept a large daily calendar in the center of her desk, and on it she scribbled everything, including appointments with clients. The calendar was not intended to be off-limits or in any way secretive; after all, it was just lying there on the desk, for anyone to see. So Theo took a look. He noticed that tomorrow, Wednesday, he had a 4:00 p.m. appointment with his orthodontist. He noticed his mother was meeting with a client named M. Clyburn.

And, at the moment, his father was meeting with a client named Joe Ford. Theo froze for a second, then he remembered his conversation with Ike the day before. Joe Ford. Also known as Fast Ford. A real estate developer; a buzzard in Ike's book who was waiting to pounce on the land around Sweeney Road in the event the bypass was approved; a shifty operator who Ike also referred to as a "thug." Theo tried to remember the other things Ike had said. The deal was for two hundred acres; it was hush-hush, secretive, and so on. Ike didn't say the deal was illegal in any way, but it certainly sounded like it.

Theo stared at the name for a few seconds. It sort of made sense. Joe Ford was in the real estate business. Woods Boone's clients were in that business. But why would Theo's father represent a man with a shady reputation?

There were voices upstairs, then heavy footsteps coming down. Theo froze for a second as he thought about disappearing. He could dart through the front door, but that would make some noise. He could duck into the conference room, or dash down the hall toward his office. As he moved, he kicked over Elsa's trash can and crumpled papers spilled onto the floor. Quickly, he bent over, scooped them up, and was trying to clean up his mess when his father and another man suddenly appeared.

"Well hello, Theo," Mr. Boone said. "What're you doing there?"

"Uh, well, Judge knocked over the trash can here, and I'm just picking up."

"Right, well, say hello to Mr. Joe Ford, one of our clients."

Mr. Ford kept his hands in his pockets and barely offered a smile.

"This is my son, Theo," Mr. Boone said proudly. "He's in the eighth grade at Strattenburg Middle School."

Theo nodded quickly and politely and said, "Nice to meet you."

"You too," Joe Ford managed to say but only because he had to. He wore a shiny gray suit, with a vest, and a starched white shirt. His hair was frizzled and permed with a couple of strands bouncing over his ears. Theo instantly disliked him and got the impression that Joe Ford didn't care for him either. Joe Ford, in Theo's quick assessment, didn't have time for anyone who could not help him make a buck.

And Mr. Ford did not believe in small talk. He excused himself and left the building. Theo hustled back to his office, clicked on his laptop, and immediately opened a file on Mr. Joe Ford.

Chapter 13

The three boys—Theo, Woody, and Hardie—along with one dog, Judge, met at Truman Park near downtown as soon as possible after school on Friday. A fishing trip had been organized, and the boys were excited about the adventure. A rough week of school had just ended and it was time to relax. Fishing had been Hardie's idea. He wanted to show Theo firsthand the Quinn family farm and the beautiful scenery the governor and some other politicians now wanted to destroy. Woody and Theo followed Hardie, with Theo bringing up the rear so Judge and his leash would not get tangled up with the other bikes. Though Judge was only a dog, he felt as if he should lead and the boys should follow. On a leash, though, he obediently trotted alongside Theo and seemed happy just to be included. They zigzagged through the shady streets of the old sections and made their way to a biking trail that looped around the southern part of town and avoided the traffic and residential areas. At a busy intersection, they crossed Highway 75 and soon disappeared down a narrow country lane with trees touching in an arc above it. The town and its congestion and noise were behind them. They sped down hills and grunted up them. They crossed tiny creeks, and, at one point, rattled through an old, abandoned covered bridge.

After thirty minutes, the boys were sweating and Judge needed some water. They paused long enough for him to step into a creek. "Just a few more minutes," Hardie said. When they had caught their breath, they took off again. They topped a hill and stopped again. Below them was a beautiful valley with a few clearings and lots of trees. Hardie pointed to the only house in view, a white structure far in the distance. "That's where my grandparents live," he said, still breathing hard.

The boys took in the scenery as they rested. Hardie pointed to his right and said, "The bypass cuts across the entire valley, one wide gash that begins over there between those two hills and goes through the tallest hill that way." His right arm swept to his left. "That's Chalk Hill, and the plan is to level it with dynamite. Just blow it up and flatten it out. Everything else gets bulldozed, then covered with asphalt. Not sure what happens to my grandparents."

"How can they do this?" Woody asked.

"Ask Theo."

Theo said, "The law gives the state the right to take anybody's land. The state has to pay for it, of course, but they still get it."

"That sucks."

"It really does," Hardie said sadly.

They rolled down the hill and minutes later came to a stop in front of the house. Hardie's grandmother, Mrs. Beverly Quinn, was waiting on the porch with a plate of walnut cookies and ice water. Hardie introduced his friends, and Judge, and she sat with them during the quick snack. Hardie's grandfather was "puttering" down at the tractor barn, according to his wife. There was no mention of the bypass—that topic seemed too awful to even consider. As Theo ate a cookie and rocked gently in an old wicker rocker, he admired the spotless painted porch, the hanging ferns, the beds of neatly tended flowers, the white picket fence along the front yard, and he tried to envision a bunch of bulldozers destroying it all. The very idea seemed grossly unfair, even cruel.

When the boys finished, they thanked her and hurried off to go fishing. In a storage shed behind the house, they found a wide selection of rods and reels, along with cane poles, tackle boxes, soccer balls, volleyballs, badminton sets, Frisbees, two canoes, four kayaks, even golf clubs. "We have a lot of fun out here," Hardie said. He claimed to have eleven cousins in the Strattenburg area, along with aunts and uncles and friends close enough to be kinfolks, and they spent a lot of time on the family farm.

They picked three rods and reels, and Hardie stuffed a small tackle box into his backpack. They were off again, flying down a narrow dirt trail that wound its way through a patch of thick woods. Ten minutes after leaving the house, they plowed to a stop at the banks of Red Creek. "This is the best spot on the farm," Hardie said as he unpacked the tackle box. "Some of the best smallmouth bass in this area." Theo unleashed his dog and Judge jumped into the water. The creek was wide and the water splashed over rocks in the distance.

"We camp here all the time," Hardie said.

"It's beautiful," Theo said. "Can we go kayaking?"

"Maybe later," Hardie said. "There are some decent rapids just around the bend there, a little too rough for a canoe. We kayak it all the time."

As an only child who lived in town, Theo was mildly envious of Hardie and his big family and this tract of land where they had so much fun. The farm was like one big adventure park but with real adventures, not fake ones.

Hardie was standing on a granite ledge, about ten feet above the water, and he had cast twice into the creek when he suddenly spotted something in the distance. "What is that?" he asked himself out loud.

"What?" asked Woody, who was nearby.

Hardie pointed and said, "Look beside those trees down the hill. Some men." Theo and Woody were climbing onto the ledge next to Hardie, whose voice left no doubt he was concerned. Sure enough, across a narrow valley that bordered the creek, there were several men milling around a pickup truck, probably a half a mile away.

"That's our property," Hardie said.

"What are they doing?" Theo asked.

"Don't know, but they shouldn't be there," Hardie said.

"We should've brought binoculars," Woody said.

"Better yet, let's go find out," Hardie said, and the boys forgot about fishing. Theo could have let it pass; the men did not appear to be doing anything wrong, but he did not understand how much the Quinn family valued their land and its privacy. The boys jumped on their bikes. "Follow me," Hardie said as they took off. Judge, soaking wet, followed Theo, who followed Woody. They went a short distance and crossed the creek on an old footbridge, one barely wide enough for bikes, then they sped along a dirt road until they approached the men.

There were four of them, three younger men with an older guy who was probably the boss. Their truck was a large, service-type vehicle with a club cab and the words STRATEGIC SURVEYS painted on the doors. Not far from the truck was the beginning of a line of stakes stuck in the ground with red ribbons tied to each top.

"What do you boys want?" the older man asked.

Hardie was off his bike and approaching the men. "What are you doing here?" he asked.

"Maybe that's none of your business, kid."

"Maybe it is. This is my family's property. Who gave you permission to be here?"

The three younger men laughed at this kid with the questions. Theo looked at them—all three were fairly large with dirty shirts and beards and the general appearance of men who lived hard and made no effort to avoid trouble.

"Don't get smart with me boy," the older man said.

"What's your name?" Hardie shot back.

"Willis. What's yours?"

"Hardie Quinn. My family has owned this land for a hundred years."

"Well congratulations," Willis said with a sneer. "Ownership is about to pass over to the state."

The other three found this funny and they laughed again, and as they did so they inched forward, closer to the rear of the truck where Willis was standing less than ten feet from Hardie. Theo took a step forward and said, "He asked you a question. Who gave you permission to come onto this land?"

"The state," Willis growled toward Theo, who quickly said, "Oh yeah, but the state doesn't own this property yet."

"A bunch of wise guys," Willis said to his men. Then to Hardie and Theo he said, "Look, boys, we're here doing some preliminary survey work for the bypass, that's all. Our company has a contract with the state and they sent us out here. Why don't you boys just relax and go on about your business? We're doing our jobs and we're not bothering anyone."

To which Hardie fired back, "You're bothering me because you don't have permission to be here."

Theo, the lawyer, quickly added, "You're trespassing, okay? And that's a criminal offense. You can go to jail for it."

The shortest of the three younger men took a step in Theo's direction and said, "Wow, a real know-it-all. You watch too much TV, kid."

"That, or maybe I just have the ability to read," Theo shot back. Shorty's face turned red and he clenched his fists. Woody stepped beside Theo, and Judge was at his feet. The situation was tense and ridiculous. Three thirteen-year-old boys and a mutt facing off against four full-grown men.

There seemed to be a stalemate. The men were not leaving, and the boys were not backing down.

Theo had an idea, one that would quickly prove to be disastrous. He reached into his pocket, removed his cell phone, and said, "I'm calling 911. We'll let the police help us out here."

Willis yelled, "Put that phone down, kid! You're not calling the police!"

Theo said, "I can call anybody I want to call. Who are you to tell me I can't call someone?"

"I said put the phone down!"

Shorty suddenly lunged for Theo. He grabbed him by the arm, shook it violently, sent Theo's phone flying into the dirt, then shoved Theo to the ground. "Stupid kid," Shorty mumbled. Woody and Hardie were startled by this act of aggression, and they stepped back.

Judge, however, never hesitated. He attacked Shorty and almost bit his leg before getting kicked away. Judge growled and hissed and darted again for Shorty, who said, "Get that dog away from me."

"Come here, Judge!" Theo said as he scrambled to his feet. At that moment, he wished Judge could have been a ninety-pound pit bull trained to attack instead of a forty-pound mutt who was afraid of cats. But he was not afraid of Shorty. In a flash, Judge attacked again, and again got kicked to the side. He barked in anger and frustration and bolted again at Shorty.

As they would soon find out, the third man's name was Larry, one of Shorty's sidekicks. Larry suddenly stepped forward with a five-foot, wooden survey stake, and as Judge again went after Shorty, Larry struck the dog on the back of the head. Theo screamed and Hardie yelled and Woody picked up a rock. In the dust and dirt and chaos and horror of the moment, Larry kept whacking away at Judge as Shorty kept kicking him and the boys attempted to react. Woody rushed forward and was tripped by the third man. He fell on top of Theo. Hardie was yelling, "Put the stick down, okay!!"

Theo finally managed to throw himself on top of Judge, and for good measure Larry popped Theo on the rear end with the stake. The men were laughing; the boys were crying; and poor little Judge was bleeding and whimpering.

The men backed away.

Theo cradled his dog and gently lifted him. He had blood all over his head and his body was limp. "Talk to me, Judge," Theo pleaded through tears.

Hardie screamed at the men, "You'll pay for this."

Theo began running. He clutched Judge to his chest and ran past his bike, because he knew he couldn't ride it and hold Judge at the same time. Hardie and Woody jumped on their bikes and soon caught up with Theo, who was jogging in a daze, tears on his cheeks, blood on his shirt, Judge close to his heart.

Hardie said, "Woody, you stay with Theo. I'll sprint ahead and get my grandfather."

"Good idea," Woody said, and Hardie was gone.

"Is he alive, Theo?" Woody asked softly as he rode as close to Theo as possible.

Theo bit his lip and said, "I don't know. He's not moving."

Blood was dripping from Theo's elbow. He was running as fast as he could.

Chapter 14

Hardie and his grandfather, Mr. Silas Quinn, found Theo and Woody as they crossed Red Creek. Theo was soaked with sweat and blood and the stress was triggering an asthmatic attack. He was pumping his inhaler as he hovered over Judge, who wasn't moving. Mr. Quinn quickly scooped up the dog and placed him on the seat of his pickup truck. "Put the bike back there and get in," he ordered, and Woody tossed his bike into the bed of the truck. The boys crowded into the front seat, with Theo gently cradling Judge, whose eyes were closed.

"Is he gonna make it?" Hardie asked his grandfather.

"He'll be all right," Mr. Quinn said as he shifted gears and took off. He had already called 911 and requested an ambulance and the police. He wanted the survey crew off his property, and he would have preferred to confront them himself. But, at the moment, there was a badly injured dog to deal with. They were flying along a gravel road, headed for town. Mr. Quinn said, "Who has a cell phone?"

Woody did not because he was only thirteen and his parents thought he was too young. Hardie had one but he wasn't sure where it was. Theo said, "I do."

"I think you should call your parents, Theo," Mr. Quinn said. Theo gently placed Judge into Woody's lap and pulled his phone out of his pocket. "Where are we going?" Theo asked.

"Not sure," Mr. Quinn said. "Who's your vet?"

"Dr. Kohl."

Elsa answered the phone at the office. She informed Theo that his mother was in a meeting with a client but his father was not. As he told his dad what happened, he gently stroked Judge between the eyes. He glanced at Woody, the toughest kid he knew, and saw tears.

They stopped the ambulance in the middle of the county road that led to the Quinn farm. At first the crew was not sure how to handle an injured dog, but Mr. Quinn was not a man to argue with. In loud and colorful language, he told the crew to take Theo and the dog to Dr. Kohl's office on South Clement Street. Mr. Quinn, Hardie, and Woody would follow in the pickup truck.

Inside the ambulance, Theo watched as the two

paramedics treated Judge as though he were a badly injured child. They placed him on a sterile white gurney, cleaned his wounds, whispered words of encouragement to him, and checked his pulse. Though it was obvious to Theo they were trained to assist humans and not dogs, they did a wonderful job of making Judge comfortable, and Theo as well. His shirt was covered with blood and dirt, and one of the paramedics slowly wiped it with gauze to make it somewhat cleaner.

"He has a pulse," the other one said as he pulled a sheet up to Judge's neck. "I think he'll be all right."

"Thanks," Theo managed to say.

"We've never hauled in a dog before," one said. "What happened to him?"

Theo just shook his head, unable to tell the story.

For almost forty years, Dr. Kohl had mended and healed most of the dogs and cats and other small animals in Strattenburg. His quiet little office was in an old shopping center that had seen better days. His long-time receptionist was Miss Ross, a fiercely efficient assistant known to call and scold clients when their pets' rabies vaccines had expired.

Miss Ross was at her desk late that Friday, making things tidy and getting ready to leave, when the phone rang and Mr. Woods Boone explained the family dog was en route and in bad shape. Was Dr. Kohl around? Indeed he was. Minutes later, Miss Ross watched in disbelief as an ambulance roared to a stop at the front door.

In forty years with Dr. Kohl, she could not remember an injured animal arriving in an ambulance. She knew Judge Boone was a special dog (weren't they all?) but had no idea he had such respect in the community. Behind the ambulance was a pickup truck, then a police car, then two other vehicles. A paramedic cradled the dog and rushed him inside. The small waiting room quickly filled with a bunch of nervous people—Theo, his buddies, his parents, Mr. Quinn, the paramedics and ambulance driver, Elsa from the office, and two officers in uniform.

While Dr. Kohl and a technician carried Judge into the back for X-rays, Theo was examined by his parents. He was covered in dirt, blood, and sweat. He was barely able to control his emotions as he told the story, with Woody and Hardie helping with the details.

"He actually struck you with the stick?" Mr. Boone said.

"Twice, on the backside," Theo answered. "And the short one knocked me down."

"One of them pushed me down too," Woody added.

"This is outrageous," Mrs. Boone said, staring at the

two policemen. One of them said, "We're on the scene, Mrs. Boone."

"I should hope so."

"We want to press charges as soon as possible," Mr. Boone said. "I want these thugs in jail."

"So do I," said Mr. Quinn. "They were on my property without permission."

The group quickly agreed that the bad guys must be brought to justice, then things settled down a bit. The waiting began. The policemen and ambulance crew signed off and disappeared. Miss Ross made a pot of coffee and they all drank it from paper cups. After about an hour, Dr. Kohl came out for his first update. He explained that Judge was alive, barely, but in bad shape. He had a faint pulse. He had taken several blows to the head and these had caused a severe concussion. There was no fracture of the skull, but quite a lot of swelling around the brain. His right front leg was broken and several teeth were knocked out. In Dr. Kohl's opinion, he was lucky to still be breathing and the next twenty-four hours would be crucial. If the brain continued to swell, Judge probably would not survive.

Dr. Kohl led Theo and his parents into the rear of the clinic, to an exam room where the lights were dimmed. On a small table covered with a sterile white sheet, Judge lay on his side, eyes closed, tongue hanging out, fur shaved from his face and head, an IV stuck to his left front leg, and a splint on his right front leg. He was such a pathetic sight that Theo immediately began crying. He couldn't help it and he couldn't stop. He hated crying, especially in front of a stranger, but, staring at his gravely wounded buddy, he just couldn't hold back the tears. Mrs. Boone was crying too.

After they gawked at Judge for a long time, Dr. Kohl said, "There is nothing else I can do. I'll have a technician here all night to monitor things, but, frankly, it's now just a matter of waiting."

"I'm not leaving," Theo said, teeth and braces clenched tightly. "I'm staying here all night."

"Come on, Theo," Mr. Boone said.

"I'm not leaving. When I'm sick, Judge stays beside my bed and never leaves. I can do the same for him. Forget it, Dad, I'm not leaving."

Mrs. Boone said, "Theo—"

"Forget it, Mom. Judge needs to hear my voice and know that I'm here. I'll talk to him all night, okay? Please."

The adults looked at each other, then Dr. Kohl shrugged. "It's up to you," he said. "Doesn't matter to me."

Mrs. Boone said, "Okay, Theo, but let's go home, have a quick dinner, take a shower, and change clothes."

"No Mom. I'm not leaving. I'll never leave Judge. Never."

Occasionally, in the chaotic game of parenting, it was important for the adults to yield and allow the kids to get their way. This seemed like a perfect moment, and Mr. and Mrs. Boone were wise enough to understand.

Mrs. Boone stepped closer and patted her son on the shoulder. "Okay, Theo, we're going to run home, get some clean clothes and something to eat, and we'll be back in an hour. Okay?"

"Thanks Mom," Theo said, without taking his eyes off Judge.

When his parents and Dr. Kohl were gone, and the door was closed, Theo leaned over Judge and gently kissed him on the nose. With tears dripping off his cheek, he began whispering into his ear. "I love you, Judge, and I'm gonna talk to you until you wake up. Okay? Listen to me, Judge, because I'll never stop talking."

But Judge never moved.

Chapter 15

It would be a long night. Mrs. Boone brought Theo a sandwich, which he could not eat, and a clean shirt and jeans. She and Mr. Boone took turns sitting in the cramped exam room with Theo and Judge. There were only two chairs, one on each side of the table where Judge clung to life. Dr. Kohl's assistant was a strange young woman named Star. She had purple hair and a ring in her nose, but in spite of first appearances, she was incredibly sweet and deeply concerned about Judge. When Dr. Kohl said good-bye around 9:00 p.m., he explained to Theo and his parents they were welcome to spend the night in the clinic, and Star would take care of things. Dr. Kohl would keep his cell phone nearby and could be at the clinic within ten minutes if something happened. The Boones thanked him repeatedly.

Out in the reception room, Woody, Hardie, and Mr. Quinn were still waiting. They had been there for hours with nothing to do but wait. They had ordered a pizza, which they had shared with Star. When Dr. Kohl left, they decided to leave too. Woody and Hardie promised Theo they would return early on Saturday morning to check on him and Judge. When they embraced for the night, all three boys had moist eyes. It had been a long, rough day.

A few minutes after they left, April Finnemore arrived with her mother, May, an unusual woman Theo and everybody else tried to avoid. Because Star refused to allow visitors back in the exam rooms, Theo had a chat with April in the front reception area. He didn't want to tell the story again but didn't have much of a choice. April was one of his best friends, and when she asked, through tears—"Theo what happened?"—he had little choice but to start with the fishing trip and finish with a badly injured dog.

Ms. Finnemore, who had a big mouth and a penchant for high drama, listened with wild eyes and her hand over her mouth, as if she had never heard of such brutality. Mrs. Boone managed to ease her off to one side so the kids could talk. Theo adored April, but he was relieved when she left with her mother.

Things changed when Uncle Ike arrived ten minutes later. He insisted on seeing Judge, and when Star objected

Ike growled at her and she ran for cover. After a visit with Judge, and a few words whispered into his ear, Ike announced he would be staying there through the night with Theo. Mr. and Mrs. Boone were to go home and get some sleep. Star could hang around if she wanted. She explained that Dr. Kohl had instructed her to monitor Judge throughout the night. Ike seemed to approve of this.

Mr. and Mrs. Boone left again, with another round of hugs and thanks to Star, and they promised to sleep with their cell phones in case something happened. Star locked the front door of the clinic and retreated to a small employees' lounge. Ike assumed a seat next to Judge and said, "Theo, it's important for Judge to hear our voices, okay? So you and I are going to talk as long as we possibly can. We're going to tell stories, take turns, make up jokes, whatever it takes to keep the words flowing, okay?"

"Sure, Ike." Theo was standing beside Judge. Ike slung his feet and sandals onto a small counter and somehow managed to get comfortable in the cheap plastic chair. He said, "Now, I want you to tell me again the story of how that stupid kid got himself bitten by the copperhead last week."

Theo frowned and said, "Come on, Ike. I'm sick of that story."

Ike said, "It's not about you, not about me, it's all about Judge. Maybe Judge wants to hear the story again.

Your voice, Theo, somewhere down deep, in the deepest part of his little wounded brain, Judge can hear your voice. He doesn't care what you're saying. What matters is that he knows you're here, next to him, talking to him."

Theo swallowed hard, and began the story of Percy and the copperhead.

Ike shook his head and interrupted. "No, no, Theo. Start at the very beginning, and go slow. We're in no hurry. Judge is in no hurry. We have hours to kill."

So Theo tried again. He started with Troop 1440 leaving on the bus, headed for Lake Marlo, and he threw in every large and small detail he could possibly remember. Ike nodded along, smiling. Attaboy.

When he finished the snake story, Ike said, "Now, Theo, we just had a big murder case here in Strattenburg, the biggest ever. What's the man's name?"

"Pete Duffy."

"Right, right. Mr. Pete Duffy, accused of killing his wife, wasn't he?"

"That's correct."

"So tell me that story, and start with the murder and how the police found the body. You watched the trial, right?"

"I did."

"Good. Tell me about it."

Theo sat in the other chair and pulled his knees to his

chest. The Pete Duffy murder case was one of his favorite subjects, and he talked about it forever, it seemed. From time to time, he glanced at Judge, who appeared to be resting quietly, motionless. Occasionally, he glanced at Ike, who was wide awake and staring and nodding at the wall. Star peeked through the open door from time to time, always with a smile, always listening not far down the hall.

When he wrapped up the last installment of the Duffy story, Ike said, "Remember that time we took off and went to rescue April Finnemore, just the two of us?"

"Of course I remember, Ike. How could I forget?"

"Okay, let's do that story."

"It's your turn, Ike. You were involved in that one."

Ike said, "Well, as I remember it, your buddy April disappeared from her home one night when no one else was there." Ike stood and stretched his legs. He did a few quick squats, cracked his knuckles, and when the blood was flowing he continued with the story. Theo added details along the way, just a few at first but after twenty minutes the two were tag-teaming as they relived their adventure of finding April and rescuing her from her crazy father.

Around midnight, Star brought them bottles of cold water and did a quick check of the patient. Judge was breathing but not awake.

Ike said, "Star, welcome to our little story time. Would

you like to play along? You can choose any story you want because Judge doesn't care. He just loves stories."

Theo wanted to hear the story of how she managed to get a ring in her nose, but knew that was probably off-limits. Star said, "Let me think about it. I'll be back in a few minutes."

"I guess she doesn't like to tell stories," Ike mumbled. "What about that time, Theo, when someone broke into your locker and planted some stolen goods? And the police were about to arrest you? Just a couple of months ago, right?"

"How could I forget?"

"And someone kept slashing your bike tires."

"That's it."

"Great. Tell Judge and me that story again."

Theo was suddenly tired. He was physically exhausted and needed sleep, and he was emotionally drained as well. He stood, did a few squats like Ike, and began the rather frightening story of being accused of a crime and nearly arrested. Ike had been involved in that story, too, and he inserted a few details along the way.

The chatter continued, and down the hall Star listened with amusement. Around 2:00 a.m., things became quiet in the exam room, and Star peeked inside. Theo was asleep in one corner, curled into an awkward position on top of a sleeping bag his father had brought. Ike had somehow managed to fall asleep sitting in a chair with his feet propped up.

She eased inside and gently touched Judge near his heart. It was still beating.

The police investigators arrived at Dr. Kohl's clinic early Saturday morning. Dr. Kohl was not yet in, but Star had unlocked the clinic and welcomed the officers. They chatted with Theo and Ike for about fifteen minutes and left. They said their plans were to talk to both Hardie and Woody that morning. Theo learned that the survey crew had disappeared by the time the police arrived yesterday afternoon, so no arrests were made. The police did retrieve Theo's bike and he could pick it up at the station. Ike made it very clear that the Boone family certainly intended to press charges, and have the men arrested and brought to justice.

Unknown to Theo, Hardie had managed to memorize the license plate number of the survey crew's truck.

Mr. and Mrs. Boone arrived with doughnuts and coffee. Ike left soon thereafter. He promised to return that afternoon. Dr. Kohl examined Judge at 9:00 a.m. and said there was little change in his condition. The fact that he had survived the night was obviously a good sign, but the veterinarian cautioned them against too much optimism. Mrs. Boone suggested Theo go home, take a shower, and get some rest, but Theo refused. He was not leaving Judge until Judge was fully awake and feeling fine.

No one argued with Theo.

Mr. Boone left but Mrs. Boone stayed at the clinic. She established herself in one corner of the reception area, opened her laptop, and began going through her e-mails. She had a thick briefcase by her side and lots of work to do. Theo sat with her for a few minutes and made small talk, then he went to check on Judge. Back and forth, back and forth. The day dragged on as sick dogs and cats came and went through the reception area. Dr. Kohl was popular because he'd been there so long, but he had also discovered that Saturday was the perfect day for business. He didn't work on Mondays, preferring instead to play golf, but on Saturdays, he was a busy vet. Once an hour, he checked on Judge.

Mr. Boone arrived and Mrs. Boone left. April returned on her bike, without her mother, and stayed with Theo for an hour. When Dr. Kohl and the technicians weren't looking, Theo sneaked her in for a quick visit with Judge. She could not hold back the tears at the sight of the patient, partially tucked under a white sheet, his head shaved, eyes closed, and little pink tongue hanging out. Theo, though, was tired of crying.

Dr. Kohl X-rayed Judge again and reported the swelling had gone neither up nor down. At 2:00 p.m., another vet, a Dr. McKenzie, arrived at the clinic. According to Dr. Kohl, Dr. McKenzie was a friend and trusted colleague and was there to examine Judge and give a second opinion. With Theo out of the exam room, the two vets poked and prodded, studied the X-rays, and seemed rather gloomy about Judge's condition.

Throughout Saturday, Theo rarely left Judge's side. His parents came and went. Vets came and went. Technicians came and went. Woody, Hardie, and April came and went. Alone with the door closed, Theo gently stroked the soft fur along his dog's back, whispering and assuring him that things were going to be fine. He watched intently as Judge's stomach rose slowly, then fell, clear proof he was still breathing, still alive. "Come on, boy," he said for the millionth time.

Judge was a mutt whose age and breeding would always be a mystery. He had been abandoned by someone and taken into custody by the city's Animal Control unit. He had been placed in a shelter, given his shots, fed and groomed, and put up for adoption, but no one wanted him. The animal rights activists in town had long been seeking a no-kill policy at the city's shelter, but the sad fact remained that there were too many stray dogs and cats and not enough people willing to adopt them. After six months in the shelter, the city had no choice but to "put down" the unwanted animals. For Judge, his six months had expired, and he was hours away from the end.

Two years earlier, when Theo was eleven, he had gone to Animal Court with his dad to help a friend whose German shepherd had bitten the mailman for the third time. Animal Court, also known as Kitty Court, among other names, was in the basement of the courthouse, and was considered by the lawyers to be the lowest possible place in the entire judicial system. In fact, most lawyers avoided Animal Court.

Judge Yeck was a part-time judge, and perhaps the only lawyer in town who wanted to fool with Animal Court. During the dispute over the German shepherd, Judge Yeck looked at Theo and said, "Say, Theo, what kind of dog do you have?"

Theo, who was sitting behind his father, was honored to be recognized by a judge, even if it was in Animal Court. He stood and said, "Well, sir, I don't have a dog."

"Why not? Every kid needs a dog." Judge Yeck looked at Mr. Boone and said, "Woods, why don't you let your kid have a dog?" Theo was thrilled and couldn't help but smile, braces and all. He had been bugging his parents about getting a dog for at least a year.

Mr. Boone looked embarrassed and said, "Well, Judge, we're talking about it."

As Theo would later learn, after he and Judge Yeck became pals, the judge loved animals and hated to see them destroyed. He looked at a bailiff and said, "Bring that mutt in here." The bailiff disappeared through a door and within seconds returned with the mutt, the one who was about to be renamed Judge.

Yeck said, "Look at this handsome dude, Theo. Wouldn't he make a great friend?"

The handsome dude looked directly at Theo, and Theo looked directly at him, and at that moment the friendship was sealed. Judge was knee-high to an adult, weighed forty pounds, had a lot of terrier and thick fur and big brown eyes and was the cutest dog Theo had ever seen.

"He sure would," Theo managed to say.

"What about it, Woods?" Judge Yeck said.

"Gee, I don't know."

"Well, here's the deal. This guy has been in the shelter for six months, the limit. He's scheduled to be put down tomorrow morning. If you guys don't take him, then it's over. Wouldn't that be a shame?"

Indeed it would. Theo left with the dog.

His father told him later that Judge Yeck was known to

pull that stunt, to bring in some poor dog or cat about to be "destroyed" and shove it off on some unsuspecting person in his courtroom. That was another reason a lot of people avoided Animal Court.

Around dark, Mrs. Boone said rather sternly it was time for Theo to go home, if only to bathe, brush his teeth, change clothes, and get something to eat. Mr. Boone agreed and they seemed determined to see this happen. Theo, however, wouldn't budge. "I'm not leaving Judge," he insisted. A brief family feud was under way when Ike strode through the front door and said, "How's old Judge?"

"Hanging in there," Theo said. "Could be a long night."

"Well, we survived last night," Ike said with a grin. "I'm sure we can pull Judge through another one."

"Are you staying?" Theo asked.

"Wouldn't miss it for the world."

Mr. and Mrs. Boone eventually left. Star returned for the night shift. Dr. Kohl examined the dog around 8:00 p.m., then said his good-byes. As always, he would be waiting by the phone.

Another long night began.

Chapter 16

At dawn on Sunday morning, two deputies knocked on the door of a small brick house in a rural part of Stratten County, near a community called Tuffsburg. The owner finally came to the door and demanded to know what was going on. When asked his name, he replied, "Larry Samson."

"Then you're under arrest," one deputy said as the other unhitched a set of handcuffs from his belt.

"For what?" Samson demanded.

"Assault. Step outside. You're going with us."

Samson argued for a few minutes, but soon backed down and surrendered, griping the entire time. The deputies suggested he shut up as they shoved him into the rear of the squad car.

At that same moment, three other men were being arrested at various points around the county. Shorty, as he was known to the boys, was actually Lester Green. The supervisor of the Strategic Surveys crew, the older guy, was Willis Keeth. The fourth guy, the one who tripped Woody, was Gino Gordon. All four were taken to the Stratten County jail, where they were processed, fingerprinted, photographed, and charged with assault and trespassing. After a couple of hours of phone calls and paperwork, they were released on bond and given dates to appear in court.

Once they were in custody, a police officer, a Captain Mulloy, drove to the vet clinic to meet with the Boones. Captain Mulloy had been around for a while and was well-known and respected, especially by the older lawyers in town. He had been monitoring the situation that began on the Quinn farm Friday afternoon and involved a badly wounded dog now fighting for his life. Captain Mulloy was also a member of the church where Hardie's father was the minister, and thus knew the Quinn family well.

Theo's father always said life in a small town can be irritating because everyone knows your business, but at the same time, it can be easier and safer because you know the right people. Captain Mulloy was one of the good guys.

He arrived at Dr. Kohl's clinic and found Mrs. Boone in the reception area, a quilt over her legs, reading the Sunday newspapers. She explained that she had been there about an hour; that Theo and his uncle Ike were back there in the exam room, where they'd spent a second night in a row; and that Dr. Kohl was expected any moment. There was no change in Judge's condition.

Captain Mulloy and Mrs. Boone drank coffee for a few minutes as he told her of the arrests. Halfway through the story, Theo and Ike appeared in the reception area. Theo, who hadn't bathed since Friday morning, looked as though he'd been sleeping on the floor, which he had. And Ike, well Ike always looked rumpled and wrinkled with his long, straggly gray hair pulled into a ponytail. After introductions, Captain Mulloy asked, "So how's the dog?"

Theo replied, "Hanging in there. A slight heartbeat, but not much else. Still unconscious."

"Sorry to hear that," Captain Mulloy said as he reached for a file. "Let me show you something." He removed four large color photos, each of a different face, and laid them on a coffee table covered with magazines. "Look at these guys, Theo. Ever seen them before?"

Theo leaned down, and within seconds said, "That's them. All four of them." He pointed to Lester (Shorty) Green and said, "He's the guy who grabbed my phone and knocked me down." He pointed to Larry Samson and said, "This is the thug who kept hitting Judge with a stick." He pointed to Willis Keeth and said, "He's the older guy, the boss." And about Gino Gordon, he said, "This is the guy who tripped Woody and was cussing at us so bad."

Captain Mulloy smiled and said, "Thought so. At this moment, these guys are downtown, under arrest and getting booked. They'll probably post a bond this morning and get out. Do you understand all this, Theo?"

Theo certainly did. He nodded and said, "Yes, sir."

Ike picked up the photo of Larry Samson and said, "This is the bad boy who tried to kill Judge?"

"That's him," Theo said, no doubt.

"So when does this jerk face a judge?"

"Not sure," Captain Mulloy said.

"He looks guilty," Ike said, spitting contempt.

"He is guilty," Theo said. "There are witnesses."

"Where do these guys live?" Mrs. Boone asked.

"Around here. They work for a survey company that was hired by the state to do some early work on the bypass. It appears as though they were a bit too eager and entered some private land without permission."

"They're gonna serve time in jail," Ike said as if he were the judge. "Mark my word, these clowns are serving time. Plus, we'll sue them for damages." Ike looked as though he was ready for a fistfight.

Mr. Boone walked through the front door with a dozen doughnuts and another stack of Sunday newspapers. Theo was always amazed at the volume of newsprint consumed by his parents on a typical Sunday. Often there were four thick newspapers scattered from the kitchen table to the den and even on the back porch in good weather. One of Theo's household chores was to organize the recycling program. In one corner of the garage he kept four large plastic bins, one each for glass, plastic, aluminum, and paper. The paper bin was always full, always overflowing with stacks of old newspapers. On several occasions he had asked his parents why they simply didn't read the news online. They owned laptops and used them for business and personal e-mails. Why not get the news online and save all that paper? Their answers were vague and unsatisfactory, at least to Theo.

He stared at the stack of Sunday newspapers and thought, *What a waste.* Then he flashed back to the present and wondered why he, Theo Boone, a boy whose dog was practically dead and a boy who'd just slept two nights on the floor in a vet clinic, was worrying about recycling old newspapers. He grabbed a doughnut and downed it in three bites.

Mr. Boone was saying hello and asking about Judge when Dr. Kohl appeared from the rear. He was wearing a suit and tie and said he was on the way to early church. The group passed around the photos of the four freshly arrested men and, with frowns, silently condemned them. Dr. Kohl said something like, "Rough bunch."

Theo had an idea. He looked at Captain Mulloy and said, "Can I borrow that photo of Larry Samson?" Captain Mulloy handed it to him. The adults watched Theo as he disappeared into the rear of the clinic.

The exam room was dark and deserted; only Judge was there, still motionless on the table where he had been for so long. Theo turned on a light and hovered over his dog. "Hey buddy," he said softly into his ear. "Got something for you." Theo held the photo of Larry Samson close for Judge to see. "This is the outlaw who did this to you, Judge. His name is Larry, and right now Larry is sitting in jail. They're gonna bust him, Judge, and make him pay. Look at him, Judge, big bad Larry, the guy with the stick who thought he was so tough, whipping a little dog, is now behind bars. We won, Judge, and we're not finished."

Theo held the photo, but Judge did not look. Theo fought back tears. The photo was shaking. Theo closed his eyes and asked God to look down on this poor little dog who'd never harmed anyone, who was the best friend in the world, who'd been badly injured trying to protect Theo. Please, God.

Minutes passed, and Theo was ready to give up.

There was a sound, sort of a weak grunt, as if Judge was trying to clear his throat. Theo opened his eyes, and at about the same time Judge opened his. Not wide, just two narrow slits, but Theo could see the dark brown irises of Judge's eyes. "Judge, you're awake!" he gushed, and leaned even lower so that his nose was about two inches from his dog's.

Judge opened his eyes wider. He seemed to look at the photo of Larry Samson, to stare at it, then he opened his mouth and licked his lips. Theo placed the photo on a table, then with both hands began rubbing along Judge's back, talking nonstop.

Dr. Kohl walked in and said, "Well, well, I guess Judge says he's not ready to go."

"Look at him!" Theo said. "He's wide awake."

"I see." Dr. Kohl gently removed a tube and gently touched the swollen places. Judge was coming to life, whimpering and trying to wiggle around. The splint on his right front leg bothered him, and he couldn't figure out why it was there. When Dr. Kohl touched it, Judge squealed and jerked away. "He'll need a painkiller."

"I bet he's starving," Theo said, unable to contain his excitement.

"No doubt, but let's get him some water first." Dr. Kohl

slowly lifted Judge and held him as he tried to stand on the table. Theo grabbed a small metal bowl, ran some water in it, and offered it to Judge, who slurped it down as if he'd never seen water before. As he drank and made a mess, and while Dr. Kohl was still helping him stand, Theo stuck his head out the door and yelled, "Judge is awake!"

Within seconds the exam room was packed as the four Boones, Dr. Kohl, Captain Mulloy, and two vet technicians gathered around to watch Judge attack the water. Dr. Kohl finally released him, and there he was—Judge Boone, alive and standing alone on three good legs and one broken one. His head was swollen and shaved and he looked as though he'd been run over by a truck, but he was happy and grinning and wondering why all those humans were crying.

The Judge was back.

Chapter 17

Animal Court. In the basement of the old, majestic, and imposing Stratten County Courthouse, there was a dusty hallway with several neglected rooms off it. On the door of the largest of these rooms was a sign that said simply: ANIMAL COURT. Inside, the room was filled with the county's leftovers—old folding chairs that were mismatched; an old battered table that the judge used as a bench; old semiretired bailiffs who drifted in from time to time; and an old grouchy clerk who was hard of hearing and despised her job. Much finer courtrooms existed on the floors above the basement, and Theo had spent time in all of them. His favorite was the main courtroom, where Judge Henry Gantry presided. He loved Animal Court, too, because you didn't have to be a lawyer to argue your case.

At the age of thirteen, Theo already had several impressive wins before Judge Yeck.

The dingy courtroom and its contents may have been old, but Judge Yeck certainly was not. He was about forty, with long hair and a beard, and he preferred blue jeans and combat boots to black robes and bow ties. He was hip and cool and Theo liked him a lot. It was only a part-time job— Judge Yeck was allowed to play judge four afternoons each week because no other lawyer in town wanted to. Animal Court was so low on the ladder no other lawyer wanted to get near it.

Theo stopped by all the time. Animal Court was open for business from 4:00 p.m. to 6:00 p.m. Tuesday through Friday, and the docket usually included an interesting case or two. Sometimes, though, business was slow, and on those occasions, Theo would pull up a chair and chat with Judge Yeck about the law, law school, other lawyers, the legal gossip around town, and especially about other trials. He sort of felt sorry for Judge Yeck because when he wasn't presiding over Animal Court he worked in a small firm that was rumored to be somewhat less than successful.

Boa constrictors, biting dogs, spitting llamas, dive-bombing parrots, mail-order pythons, rabid cats, wayward monkeys, potbellied pigs, deadly spiders, de-scented skunks, wounded mountain lions, abandoned baby crocodiles,

illegal fighting chickens, hungry bears, a demented moose—
Animal Court and Judge Yeck had seen it all.

But he had never seen a crowd as large as this. At 5:00
p.m. Wednesday, his courtroom was packed, and the mood
was tense. On one side there were the Boones—Mr. and
Mrs. Boone, both fine lawyers in town—and between them
sat young Theo. On the floor beside Theo was a familiar
face, though the face, swollen and bandaged, looked a bit
different. The mutt had been renamed Judge, in honor of
Judge Yeck, according to Theo, though Judge Yeck had heard
the gossip that young Theo had remarked to several other
judges that he had named his dog in their honor. Directly
behind Theo was Ike Boone, a once prominent lawyer in
Strattenburg who had fallen hard years earlier.

Crowded together behind the Boones were a number of
friends. Woody, his parents, and two of his older brothers.
Hardie Quinn, his parents, his grandparents, and several
of his aunts, uncles, and cousins. Several of Theo's friends
from school, including Chase and April, along with her
crazy mother. Mr. Mount was there for support, along with
Captain Mulloy. Dr. Kohl and Star were there, in case they
needed to testify about Judge's injuries. Elsa from the office
sat next to Dr. Kohl. Along the back two rows were some of
the courthouse regulars who tried not to miss a good fight.

On the other side of the courtroom, sitting shoulder

to shoulder and offering frowns and scowls that left no doubt they hated where they were at that moment, were the four men who had been arrested Sunday morning. The four men from Strategic Surveys—Larry Samson, Lester Green, Willis Keeth, and Gino Gordon. Seated behind them were wives and girlfriends, family members and others. Seated in front of them was a hotshot lawyer named Mora Caffrey, also known in some places as More Caffeine, due to her aggressive nature, jerky actions, and quick tongue. Like most lawyers in town, she had no desire to be seen in Animal Court.

Placed between the two groups were two young deputies, armed and in uniform. Judge Yeck thought the case might get tense, and so he asked for more security.

Judge Yeck said, "All right, the next case involves some complicated issues. I think I understand the background facts and most of the charges. As of today, the four employees of Strategic Surveys—Samson, Green, Keeth, and Gordon—are facing criminal charges of assault, assault on a minor, and trespassing. These charges will be dealt with in Circuit Court, not here. I understand there is also a civil suit that was filed this morning by Mr. Silas Quinn against these four men and their employer. Again, that's another fight for another day in another courtroom."

Judge Yeck paused and looked around the crowded room. "This court has jurisdiction over animals and animals only. By law, that includes issues involving cruelty to animals. I'm looking at a complaint filed by Mr. Theodore Boone in which he alleges that Mr. Larry Samson took a five-foot wooden survey stake and beat his dog, Judge, until he was unconscious. That sounds like cruelty to me, so I am assuming authority over this case. Any response, Ms. Caffrey?"

Ms. Caffrey stood with her legal pad and her reading glasses perched on the tip of her nose and said, "Your Honor, we have filed a motion to dismiss these charges, or, in the alternative, to move everything to Circuit Court."

To which Judge Yeck rudely said, "Motion denied. And you don't have to stand up in my court. Anything else?"

Theo had seen this before. Hotshot lawyers appearing before Judge Yeck with an attitude because they considered Animal Court to be the bush leagues. They usually did not fare too well.

Ms. Caffrey sat down and said, "Yes, Your Honor, we would like a record of this trial, so we brought along a court reporter."

"Sure," Judge Yeck said with a shrug. Animal Court was not a court of record, which meant that the testimony of the witnesses and the statements of the judge and lawyers were not recorded in any way. In every other court in the building, a court reporter, or stenographer, recorded everything electronically and by shorthand. Because the altercation between the boys, Judge, and the survey crew had led to so many legal problems, it was a wise move to start recording the testimony of the witnesses.

"Anything else?" Judge Yeck asked Ms. Caffrey.

"Yes, Your Honor, I ask that you recuse yourself as judge in this matter and the case be assigned to another judge."

Yeck didn't flinch. "On what grounds?"

"I believe this particular dog passed through this court about two years ago, and that you were responsible for him being adopted by the Boone family."

"Why is that a problem? Who else would handle such a matter?"

"It's just, that, well, it appears as though you might be too close to this dog."

"I haven't seen this dog in two years," Judge Yeck replied. "And during that period of time a thousand dogs have come through my court. Request denied. Can we start now?" It was evident to Ms. Caffrey, and to everyone else in the courtroom, that she was already on the judge's bad side. Things could only get worse.

Ms. Caffrey did not respond.

"Anything else?" Judge Yeck asked sternly.

She shook her head. No.

Judge Yeck said, "Mrs. Boone, I believe you are acting as the attorney for your son, the owner of the dog, and that your co-counsel is Mr. Woods Boone. Correct?"

"That's correct, Your Honor," Mrs. Boone said with a warm smile.

"Then call your first witness."

Mrs. Boone said, "Theodore Boone." Theo stood, walked ten steps, and sat in an old chair closer to the judge, who said, "Raise your right hand, Theo." Theo did so, and the judge asked, "Do you swear to tell the truth?"

"I do."

Judge Yeck said, "Look, Theo, I know you've been in my court before, but today it's a little different. That court reporter over there will record every word, so I want you to speak clearly and slowly, okay? This goes for all the witnesses."

"Yes sir," Theo said.

"Proceed, Mrs. Boone."

Staying in her chair, Mrs. Boone said, "Okay, Theo, tell the court what happened."

Slowly, and as clearly as possible, Theo told the story of the encounter with the survey crew. He pointed straight at

Larry Samson when he described the beating of Judge. He almost got choked up when he described how he scooped up his bleeding and knocked-out dog and began running, and while he was running away, he heard the men laughing behind him. He looked at Judge as he testified, and he looked at his mother, father, Ike, his friends, and occasionally at the four men, all of whom sat with their arms folded over their chests. A time or two Larry Samson frowned and shook his head as if Theo were lying.

He told his story without interruption, and when he finished Ms. Caffrey declined the opportunity to question him.

Hardie went next, then Woody. All three told the same story; all told the truth. The courtroom was quiet as they testified, and Judge Yeck absorbed every word.

"Any more witnesses, Mrs. Boone?" he asked.

"Not at this time. Maybe later."

"Very well. Ms. Caffrey, call your first witness."

Without standing, she said, "Your Honor, I call the defendant, Mr. Larry Samson." As the witness stood and sort of stomped toward the front, Judge slowly rose from the floor and balanced himself on his three good legs and the broken one. He uttered a low growl, just loud enough for Theo and Ike to hear. Theo reached down and patted his back and hissed, "Shhhh." Judge relaxed but kept his eyes fixed on Mr. Larry Samson, as if he would attack and draw blood if he were able.

Mr. Samson took the witness chair, promised to tell the truth, then almost immediately started lying. After establishing where he lived and worked, Ms. Caffrey said, "So, Mr. Samson, you've heard what these three boys said. Tell us your version of what happened."

With a smirk, his first words were, "These kids are lying, all three of them. It was Friday afternoon, and after a hard week we were winding down. All of a sudden, these three kids show up on their bikes, with the dog, and start threatening us. That one there in the blue shirt, Hardie, he's the big shot and says we're on his family's land and so on, and he demands that we leave immediately. You know, we were leaving anyway, the day was over, the week was over, but anyway this smart-mouthed kid is giving us a load of crap about being on his family's property. Then the Boone kid pops off about getting us arrested for trespassing. They were jawing, we were jawing, but we weren't about to get into a fight with a bunch of little brats. Then Boone pulls out a cell phone to call the cops and we yell some more. Finally, we tell the boys we're leaving anyway and they get back on their bikes. The dog had been sniffing around, growling and such, trying to act bad, and anyway when they take off on their bikes, the dog somehow got in the way and one of the boys ran over the mutt with his bike. I didn't see it but I heard the dog squeal, and when I turned around there was a pileup with the bikes and boys and somewhere at the bottom was the dog, who was yelping pretty bad. That's how the dog got hurt."

Theo looked like he'd been kicked in the stomach. From behind him he heard gasps from Woody and Hardie. The entire Boone side of the courtroom seemed stunned, almost too stunned to think for a second or two.

Their reactions were not missed by Judge Yeck.

When Mrs. Boone finally caught her breath, she said, "So, Mr. Samson, you did not hit the dog or touch the dog in any way?"

"I did not."

She nodded suspiciously and looked directly at Judge Yeck. At this point, she could attempt to argue and haggle with the witness, but she was too experienced. Because she spent so much time in court, Mrs. Boone knew what was coming. The four men concocted a lie, which all four would stick to. Judge Yeck would have to decide which story to believe, and Mrs. Boone had a hunch he would side with Theo.

"Nothing else," she said. Theo leaned over and whispered,

"Mom, he's lying." She just nodded. Woody leaned over to his father and whispered, "Dad, he's lying." Hardie leaned over to his grandfather and whispered, "Pops, he's lying."

"Call your next witness," Judge Yeck said. As Willis Keeth walked forward, Judge Yeck glanced down at Theo and gave him a quick wink. No one saw it but Theo.

Mr. Keeth acknowledged he was the supervisor but did not want to talk about whether he had taken his crew onto someone's private property without permission. The trespassing issue would be settled in another court. As to the injured dog, he told the same story as Larry Samson. No stick, no repeated blows, no real contact or controversy with the animal. The poor dog somehow got tangled up and was run over by one or more of the bikes. He didn't see it all and was perfectly vague on certain details. Mrs. Boone tried to pin him down on exactly where he was standing during the confrontation, but Mr. Keeth had a bad memory.

More lying continued with Lester Green, though his memory was even worse than his boss's. But, he stuck to their story and placed all blame for Judge's injuries on a bad bike wreck. As he finished, Judge Yeck, who had been growing visibly frustrated, sent a chill through the courtroom when he asked Mr. Green, "Sir, do you know what perjury means?"

The witness looked confused, lost, then a bit frightened.

The judge helped him along by saying, "Perjury, Mr. Green, is when a witness lies on the stand after being sworn to tell the truth. Understand?"

"I guess so."

"Good, now do you know the penalty for perjury in this state?"

"Not really."

"Didn't think so. The penalty is whatever I want it to be, up to twelve months in jail. Did your lawyer explain this to you?"

"No sir."

"Didn't think so. You may return to your seat."

The brief perjury discussion sent ripples of fear through the other side of the courtroom. Larry Samson, Willis Keeth, and Lester Green all exchanged nervous looks. Ms. Caffrey was lost in her note taking.

Mr. Boone leaned down to Theo and said, "They're going to jail."

Judge heard this and flicked his ears.

"Call your next witness, Ms. Caffrey," Judge Yeck said gruffly.

"Mr. Gino Gordon."

Mr. Gino Gordon suddenly had no desire to testify. He had trouble getting out of his chair, had trouble walking only a few feet to the witness chair, and had trouble settling himself into it. If ever a witness wanted to flee a courtroom, it was Gino Gordon.

"Do you swear to tell the truth?" Judge Yeck asked.

"I guess."

"Yes or no, Mr. Gordon?"

"Okay, yes."

"Now, before you get started, do you know what perjury means?" Judge Yeck's rising tone and sarcastic voice left no doubt he believed Gordon was about to lie, just like the rest of his crew.

"Yes, I do," he replied, his eyes dancing around nervously.

"And do you understand you can go to jail for perjury?"

Before he could answer, Ms. Caffrey said, angrily, "Judge, please, he hasn't said anything yet."

"I get that," Yeck shot back. "Let's just say that I'm warning him, okay? Proceed."

Ms. Caffrey said, "Mr. Gordon, will you tell the court what happened?"

Mr. Gordon looked as though he was suddenly paralyzed from the neck down, with only the muscles in his face able to move. They formed a painful frown, one of complete confusion. He tried to speak, but nothing came out. He glared at Ms. Caffrey, but she was looking for something in her briefcase.

If he told a lie, he might go to jail. If he told the truth, his buddy Larry might get convicted, and his boss might fire him. He was finally able to mumble, "Well, Judge, I really didn't see anything."

Judge Yeck anticipated this and retorted, "But all three boys said you were right there. How could you miss it? Are you being truthful?"

"Well, you see, Judge, I really don't want to testify."

"Smart man. Go back to your seat."

The main door opened and two more deputies marched in and found chairs.

"Any more witnesses, Ms. Caffrey?"

"No, Your Honor."

"Mrs. Boone?"

"Yes, Your Honor, we would like to call Dr. Neal Kohl to the stand. He's the vet who treated Judge."

Dr. Kohl came forward and was sworn in. Mrs. Boone asked him to describe the injuries. Slowly and with great detail, Dr. Kohl testified that Judge suffered multiple wounds to the top, sides, and back of his head, as well as two more along the top of his spine. And, of course, a broken right front leg.

Mrs. Boone said, "You've heard the witnesses, Dr. Kohl. What caused the injuries? Repeated blows from a stick of wood, or the rubber tires of a bicycle?"

"I object," Ms. Caffrey said.

"Overruled. Please answer, Dr. Kohl."

Dr. Kohl smiled, took a deep breath, and said, "It's absurd to claim the dog's injuries were the result of being run over by a bicycle. He was injured by several hard blows from a blunt instrument."

Judge Yeck looked at Ms. Caffrey, but she had nothing else. "Thank you, Dr. Kohl. Please step down. Anything else from the lawyers? Any more witnesses?" Judge Yeck looked at his watch and continued, "We've been here almost two hours. Anybody got anything else they want to say before I make my ruling?"

No one volunteered. On the Boone side, there was the general feeling that enough had been said, and across the aisle there was nothing but fear.

Judge Yeck looked at the court reporter and said, "On the record, please. I am presented with two very different versions of what happened. The three boys tell one story, the three crew members tell another. The truth is usually somewhere in the middle, but not in this case. I believe the boys, and I believe the crew members—Mr. Samson, Mr. Keeth, and Mr. Green—created a story designed to keep them out of trouble." He glared at the men, and continued: "I think you decided you could walk into this little courtroom, into Animal Court, and simply tell your lies and all would be well. You're grown men; therefore, the court would certainly believe you before it would believe a bunch of kids. That is unfortunate. Lying is lying, regardless of who does it, and when you lie under oath in a court of law you undermine our judicial system. You, Mr. Samson, I find guilty of cruelty to animals, a Class Three offense because it involves the intentional infliction of injury. For that, I sentence you to six months in jail."

Samson yelled, "Six months! Are you kidding me?"

"No. Would you like more?"

"You're crazy!" Samson yelled again, and seemed ready to attack the bench. Two deputies stood quickly and lurked nearby. Behind Samson, his wife began sobbing. "I got a wife and kids!" he yelled.

"Quiet, Mr. Samson," Judge Yeck demanded. "I'm not finished. I also find you guilty of perjury, and sentence you to sixty days in jail, in addition to the six months."

"This ain't Animal Court, this is kangaroo court," Samson hissed.

"Get him outta here," Judge Yeck said to the deputies, who grabbed Samson, slapped on handcuffs, and half dragged him away. When the door slammed, Judge Yeck glared at Willis Keeth and Lester Green, both of whom were wide-eyed and pale. He took a deep breath—they weren't breathing—and said, "As for Mr. Gordon, you were wise enough to clam up and not testify, so you'll not be going to jail tonight. Mr. Keeth and Mr. Green will not be so lucky. I find you guilty of perjury and sentence you to sixty days in jail."

"We'll appeal," Ms. Caffrey said.

"You have that right, but as of now they're headed to jail. Take them away."

The deputies hurried around Keeth and Green. When the handcuffs were in place, they led them away.

As they walked past, Judge was on all fours, growling as loudly as possible.

Chapter 18

As was now the custom, Judge slept on the end of Theo's bed, as opposed to sleeping under it. As Judge tossed and turned through the night, he sometimes whimpered when his wounds ached. Theo could usually talk him back to sleep. Judge was mending rapidly and enjoying the attention. Theo was not sleeping too well but didn't care. He would never again fuss at his dog over anything.

On the Thursday morning after Animal Court, Theo carried Judge downstairs and released him into the backyard. Mrs. Boone was sitting at the kitchen table in her night robe, sipping coffee and reading the newspaper. "Front page," she said, and handed Theo the *Strattenburg Gazette*.

At the bottom of the front page, a bold headline read, SURVEY CREW THROWN IN JAIL. And in the center of the article was a photo of Theo holding Judge as they left court. In the excitement of the moment, Theo had been vaguely aware of a reporter and a photographer.

"Wow," he said as he admired the photo. The caption under it read, THEODORE BOONE, WITH DOG, JUDGE, SAYS HE PLANS TO FIGHT THE BYPASS AND ALL THE THUGS WHO WORK FOR IT.

"Did you really say that?" his mother asked.

"I guess I did."

"Seems a bit strong, doesn't it?"

"Maybe." Theo read the article. There were quotes from both parents, Mora Caffrey, Judge Yeck, and Larry Samson. All in all, it was an accurate account of what happened. The defendants disagreed with the verdicts and planned to appeal. Ms. Caffrey promised to have her clients out of jail by noon Thursday. Mr. Silas Quinn said he had filed a civil lawsuit against the four men and their company, and so on. Nothing new, really, except a rather nice photo of Theo and Judge on the front page. Theo liked it.

"You shouldn't have called them thugs," Mrs. Boone said.

"Why not? They're thugs, right? They trespassed and they beat my dog with a stick. They're not exactly nice guys."

"You gotta be careful around reporters, Theo. They're always ready to pounce on the wrong word. Especially Norris Flay."

"Who's Norris Flay?"

"The guy you spoke to. The guy who wrote the article. He's been around a long time and knows how to spin a story. If there's a hot issue in town, Norris Flay will be there."

"Isn't that his job?"

"Yes, it certainly is. But he doesn't always get things right."

Theo opened the back door and retrieved his dog. Judge was ready for breakfast. Theo fixed two bowls of cereal and placed one on the floor next to his chair.

Mrs. Boone sipped her coffee and said, "Your father is not too happy about this. He doesn't want you involved in the bypass fight."

"Didn't know I was involved."

"It appears you are now. You're on the front page vowing to fight the bypass."

"Why does Dad care?"

"It's a nasty political fight and no place for a kid."

"Mom, are you telling me to butt out?"

"What are your plans, Theo?"

"I have no plans." Theo took a bite of Cheerios and crunched as loudly as possible. "Do you know a man by the name of Joe Ford?" he asked as he swallowed.

"Yes, Mr. Ford has been a client of our firm for many years. Your father has done a lot of legal work for him. Why do you ask?"

"There is a rumor that he has a secret deal to purchase two hundred acres at the spot where the bypass will intersect with Sweeney Road. So if the bypass gets approved and built, Mr. Ford, who I think is also known by his nickname of Fast Ford, will be in a good position to develop the land and make a fortune."

Mrs. Boone was frowning and nodding, not sure how to respond.

Theo pressed on, "And there is another rumor, though I think it's more of a fact than a rumor, that Mr. Ford was a big contributor to the governor's last campaign. So it looks to me like Mr. Ford gives money to the governor, and the governor pushes the bypass so Mr. Ford can make even more money and then give some more back to the governor. Does this make sense, Mom?"

"This would not surprise me."

"If it's true, it sounds pretty sleazy, right Mom?"

"It's not illegal," she said, rather lamely, in Theo's opinion.

"But can't you agree that it sounds sleazy?"

"Sort of, yes."

"Then why are we mixed up in it?"

"We?"

"Yes. Why does our law firm represent sleazy clients?"

"Our law firm? Didn't realize you were now a partner."

"It's got my name on it," Theo said, then flashed his mother a metallic smile.

"Theo, we've had this discussion. Everyone has the right to a lawyer, and we, as lawyers, cannot always pick and choose our clients. Often our clients are wrong or they have done bad things, and that's why they need us. A lawyer is not supposed to judge his or her client. We are supposed to help them."

"I'm not going to represent crooks," Theo said, then took another spoonful.

Her eyebrows pinched almost together and she said sternly, "Do not refer to Mr. Ford as a crook."

"I didn't call him a crook," Theo said, chomping. "I just said that when I'm a lawyer I'm not going to have crooks as clients."

Mrs. Boone took a deep breath and decided to let the conversation die. Theo was tired of it too. He and Judge finished eating in silence.

During homeroom, Mr. Mount pulled out the morning paper and passed it around. Theo was often amazed at how few of his classmates ever looked at a newspaper, and virtually none of the other fifteen boys had seen the story. A few had scanned it online. Judge's beating and near-death experience had been a hot topic all week, and the class wanted the details from Animal Court. The front-page story and photo were inspected closely and discussed at length. Theo tried to downplay it all, but secretly thought it was way cool to be on the front page. Woody, seldom quiet, had his version of the trial, and, not surprisingly, it soon grew into something different from Theo's.

Woody's parents had filed assault charges against Gino Gordon, the only one of the four still not in jail, and Woody couldn't wait until his day in court. Hardie's parents had filed trespassing charges, both in criminal and civil courts, so the three boys were in for a full year of legal adventures. Theo thought this was wonderful, as did Mr. Mount, and the ten minutes in homeroom were again consumed with chatter about the case and its issues.

Hardie was in a different homeroom. He found Theo during the lunch break, and they had a grand time rehashing their great victory in Animal Court. The entire Quinn family was thrilled with the outcome and very proud of Theo for his role in it. They were also delighted that the kid on the front page with the bandaged dog had vowed to ". . . fight the bypass and the thugs who work for it."

"Did you really say that, Theo?" Hardie asked. The truth was, Theo wasn't sure what he'd said. As the crowd left the courtroom and spilled into the narrow hallway, there was a crush of people and a lot of talking. Theo was sort of choked up and excited; he was also stunned to see the three men hauled away in handcuffs; and he was holding Judge and just wanted to get away. He caught a glimpse of someone with a camera, and he remembered the reporter asking him some questions as he walked up the stairs.

But, it was also true that Theo really liked the quote, so he said, "Sure."

"That's awesome, Theo."

Hardie wanted to stop by the law office after school and talk about the bypass, and Theo promised to be there, in his office, doing his homework.

That's where he was at 4:00 p.m. when his father tapped on his door and said, "Follow me." Theo knew from experience this was a bad sign. His father rarely made the trek back through the storage files and cluttered rooms to Theo's office, and he never said simply, "Follow me."

They walked to the large conference room, where his father closed all the doors, then pointed to a chair for Theo to sit in. He sat in one nearby, and by the time they were seated Theo knew bad news was on the way.

Mr. Boone began, "Last week, I believe you met Mr. Joe Ford here in the office. He's been a client of mine for many years. Unfortunately, that has now ended. I received a call from Mr. Ford this morning in which he informed me he was basically firing me as his lawyer. He doesn't like the fact that my son is such a vocal opponent of the bypass. Mr. Ford is a long-time supporter of that project. Like a lot of people, he thinks it's important for our community."

Theo wasn't sure how to react. He felt lousy because his father got fired. He felt relieved Mr. Ford was gone. He thought it was an overreaction by Mr. Ford. He wanted to ask his father why he represented shady guys like Fast Ford. He decided to play it safe and said, "Sorry, Dad."

"Your mother tells me you think Mr. Ford is, shall we say, less than honest."

Thanks Mom. We can't even have a chat over breakfast without you blabbing it all to Dad. "I barely met him, Dad, so I don't know him. Is he less than honest?"

Mr. Boone smiled and glanced away. Then he said, "I've never seen anything dishonest from Joe Ford. I will say that he knows how to play the system. He has a lot of money and powerful friends, and he's accustomed to getting what he wants. He demands loyalty, and that's why he's looking for another lawyer right now."

Theo blurted, "He sounds like a crook to me."

"He's not a crook, Theo, and you need to stop throwing around words like crooks and thugs, okay?"

His father was right about this, so Theo said, "Yes, sir."

After a pause, his father asked, "Who told you about the two-hundred-acre purchase at Sweeney Road?"

Ike had told him, but Theo knew better than to admit this. He crossed his arms over his chest, clenched his teeth, and said, "I promised not to tell." This always worked since both parents knew the importance of keeping secrets.

"You haven't been snooping around this office, have you?"

Theo managed to act surprised at the very idea. "No sir. I don't snoop around this office." This was only partially true, and both he and his father knew it. To help clear things up a bit he said, "Someone told me."

Mr. Boone shook his head as if he believed this when in fact he did not, and Theo knew it.

"What else did this someone tell you?" Mr. Boone asked.

Theo had nothing to gain by saying anything else. "That's it. Nothing else."

His father's concern only confirmed the truth about Joe Ford and his shady deal, but Theo decided to leave it alone. Fast Ford had said good-bye as a client, and Theo was secretly thrilled such a bad character was gone from Boone & Boone. And he suspected he wasn't alone. Theo had a hunch his mother was on his side. She had no fondness for real estate developers in town who sought to chew up the land and build more shopping centers and condos. Things had been said before, around the office and around the house, sharp little one-liners and zingers that left no doubt Mrs. Boone did not care for some of Mr. Boone's clients. Theo was not supposed to hear these things, but Theo missed little.

Theo said, "Look, Dad, I'm sorry, but I didn't ask for any of this. I didn't ask for Judge to get hurt. I didn't ask for the trial yesterday. I didn't ask to get my photo on the front page. It all just sort of happened, and if Mr. Ford is angry, then I'm sorry. Frankly, I think he overreacted by firing our law firm."

"Our law firm?"

"Got my name on it."

Mr. Boone smiled and seemed to relax. Theo suspected he wasn't really that upset at losing Joe Ford as a client. "Go finish your homework," he said as he got to his feet.

"Sure, Dad."

Chapter 19

Theo was hard at work memorizing Spanish verbs when someone knocked on his door. It was Hardie. He stepped inside, paused to rub Judge on the head and speak to him, then said, "Say, Theo, are you free for about thirty minutes?"

On a typical afternoon, after Theo checked in at the office, he was free to come and go, as long as his homework was finished. "Sure. What's up?"

"Let's hop on our bikes, take a ten-minute ride. I want to show you something."

"What?"

"It's a surprise."

Eight minutes later, they wheeled to a stop in front of an old, redbrick warehouse in the Delmont section of town, near Stratten College. Most of the warehouses appeared to be abandoned, but on the street front there were a few offices. Above one a sign read: STRATTEN ENVIRONMENTAL COUNCIL.

"In here," Hardie said, and they walked through the front door. The SEC office was one long, wide room with high rafters, bare brick walls, and a concrete floor in serious need of sweeping. There were some desks and tables, lots of computers, aerial photos and maps tacked to the walls, and at least half a dozen dogs. Evidently, if you worked at SEC you could bring your dog to work. The place hummed with energy, and, for the most part, the crowd was young. Lots of beards and flannel shirts with faded jeans.

The Reverend Charles Quinn, Hardie's father, was in the midst of a serious conversation when he looked over and saw Theo. Loudly, he said, "Theo Boone, the man!" Others heard this and before Theo knew what was happening he was led, or sort of shoved, to a large wall. Tacked to it was the photo in the morning paper, except it had been enlarged many times over. It was gigantic, larger than life-size, and Theo was stunned to see himself and his dog blown up to the point that they covered an entire wall. His partial statement, "*. . . fight the bypass and all the thugs who work for it,*" was highlighted in bold letters and stretched across the top of the photo. While Theo was gawking at the wall, the room became quiet and the crowd gathered around him.

Reverend Quinn said to the others, "I'd like to introduce to everyone Mr. Theodore Boone, the hero of the moment, the owner of the most famous dog in town, and a great friend of my son, Hardie." Theo nodded awkwardly at the others. He would soon learn that only a handful of these people actually worked at the SEC. Most were volunteers, with the majority being students from Stratten College.

A man named Sebastian Ryan stepped forward and shook Theo's hand. He said, "I'm the director of the SEC and we're delighted to have you join us here." Theo was not aware that he had joined anything. He was suddenly very uncomfortable being the center of attention in a place he'd never been before. He said something like, "Yeah, sure, nice to meet you."

"How's the dog?" someone asked from the crowd.

"Doing great," Theo said.

"We'd like to meet him," someone else said.

"He's not traveling much these days," Theo said, and several thought it was funny. Others began drifting away. "Let's get back to work," Sebastian said, and the crowd broke up. Theo and Hardie followed Sebastian to the rear of the long room, where he had an open office tucked into a small wing. His desk had once been a wooden door but was now mounted on two cable spool pedestals, and, in Theo's opinion, was perhaps the coolest desk he'd ever seen. There were no chairs around it, and Theo had already noticed that everyone at SEC worked standing up. No sitting. He made a mental note to ask his mother about this. Probably some new fad.

Theo and Hardie stood and looked at the brick walls, all of which were covered with photos, diplomas, and maps. The first thing Theo saw was a diploma from the Stanford School of Law. Sebastian Ryan was young, perhaps not yet forty, and with his jeans, boots, and beard looked more like a hunting guide than an environmental lawyer.

He said, "I hear both of your parents are lawyers, Theo."

Theo nodded.

"And I hear you're a pretty good lawyer yourself."

"Not yet," Theo said.

"He knows a lot of law," Hardie added.

Sebastian was nervous and intense and not much for small talk. "We are attacking this bypass on many fronts. Abuse of eminent domain, destruction of natural resources, noise, pollution, an idiotic traffic plan, and so on. I have a wild idea that I'd like to share with you guys."

Theo and Hardie nodded because they really had no choice.

Sebastian walked to the wall on his left and pointed to a large map of the proposed bypass. He pointed closer and said, "This is Jackson Elementary School, prekindergarten through grade five. Four hundred students. Right now it sits off to itself, isolated from traffic and noise, just minding its own business, educating little kids while the birds chirp outside and the breeze blows the leaves here and there. However, economic development is on the way. The bypass rips through this parking lot here and comes to within a hundred yards of the school's front door. So in two years there will be four lanes of heavy traffic, big trucks and buses blasting diesel fumes into the air while cars fly by doing eighty miles an hour. It's a disaster, and the sad part is that no one has carefully studied the impact the bypass will have on the health of these kids. The governor doesn't have a clue, nor do his people. The state highway department hasn't studied it. We're raising money right now to hire experts who can analyze it and make predictions, but money is tight."

Theo doubted he and Hardie were expected to write big checks. He asked, "Where do we fit in?"

"Organize the kids. They're too young for Facebook, but they have older brothers and sisters. Four hundred students equals about three hundred families—some have more than one at the school. Organize the kids, the parents, the teachers. I like the idea of kids—you two—getting other kids involved and angry. If the kids get mad, then the parents get mad, and, of course, the parents are the voters. It's all coming down to politics. What do you think?"

Theo and Hardie were frowning at the map, not sure what to say.

Sebastian never waited long for an answer. "And it gets better," he said, taking a step to the side and pointing at the county's new soccer complex near Jackson Elementary. "Look at this, the SSC—Stratten Soccer Complex. Opened two years ago and the site of ten new fields, all with lights."

"I play there," Hardie said.

"Do you know how many kids play soccer in this area?"

"About a million," Theo said.

"A lot. Now, the bypass shaves off only three of the fields here on the eastern side, and, of course, the promise is that these fields will simply be relocated over on the western side. Two problems with that. First, you can't believe any of the promises being made. Second, the state does not yet own the property where it's promising to put these three fields. But let's say the state keeps its word and relocates the three fields. That means on any afternoon from March through October there will be several hundred kids, parents, coaches, and other spectators at the complex trying to enjoy the games with four lanes of traffic roaring by."

"So we organize the soccer kids too," Theo said.

"Exactly. Thousands of them. Get the soccer crowd upset, and our five county commissioners will run for cover."

"It's that easy?" Theo asked.

"No, it's not. Keep in mind, Theo, that a lot of folks who live here are in favor of the bypass. They're tired of the traffic on Battle Street and they think this is the solution. Any bypass is a good bypass. Heard that?"

"Yes. I read it in the newspaper."

"It's not uncommon."

Sebastian stepped away from the map and rested his rear end on his desk. He said, "The idea here, guys, is for the kids in this community to get mad, involved, and vocal. On the one hand, you have the big guys—the politicians, the trucking companies, the contractors, the businessmen who write big checks to the politicians—and on the other hand you have a bunch of kids who are about to get run over. It could be a great story, and, frankly, we need all the help we can get. This is an uphill fight, and the big money is against us. The public hearing is next month, and we're working around the clock."

"When will the commissioners vote?" Hardie asked.

"At the public hearing. They're not talking much, but it looks like two are in favor of the bypass, one is opposed, and the other two are undecided. But who knows what these guys will do. Frankly, right now, I'm not that optimistic." His cell phone vibrated. He yanked it out of his pocket, looked at it, and decided not to answer. Then his desk phone began buzzing, and he ignored that too.

Theo loved this guy. He was a lawyer, a tough cool guy with an important job and a passion for saving the environment. He seemed fearless, ready for a good fight, ready to take on the big boys. Even his office was cool, so unlike the rather stuffy ones at Boone & Boone.

Sebastian said, "We need your help, guys. Whatta you say? You can make a real difference here if you jump in and start fighting. We're on the same team."

Hardie looked at Theo, who looked at Sebastian, who was nodding as if to say, "Are you guys tough enough?"

"I'm ready," Hardie said.

"How about it, Theo?" Sebastian said. "They've already tried to kill your dog."

Theo flashed back to the nightmare of Judge being pounded with a stick, and bleeding, and looking up at Theo with those painful, frightened eyes. Theo thought about his dog, and he thought about the Quinn family and their beloved farm, and the more he thought the more determined he became. He looked at Hardie, then he glared at Sebastian, gritted his teeth, and said, "I'm in."

"All right!" Sebastian said as he slapped him on the shoulder.

At precisely 7:00 p.m. on Thursday evening, the three Boones plus Judge sat down for dinner. As always, on Thursdays, it was a roasted chicken from a Turkish deli, served with hummus, pita bread, and, tonight, couscous.

It was not Theo's favorite meal of the week. Judge, however, loved the chicken. He seemed to be improving by the hour, moving around more and sleeping less.

Mrs. Boone asked, "Theo, where did you get off to this afternoon?"

Theo anticipated this. Someone in the law firm usually noticed if he came and went, and that was usually Elsa. She could be on the phone with two lines holding, and chatting with a client at the front door, and reading e-mails on her screen, all at the same time, and still know precisely when Theo sneaked out the back door. He swallowed hard and said, "Hardie and I rode over to the Stratten Environmental Council."

His mother was intrigued and said, "Oh really."

His father frowned and said, "Why'd you go there?"

Theo said, "Hardie's father was there and he wanted me to stop by. On a wall, they have this huge blowup of the photo of Judge and me leaving court last night."

"So you're the hero?" his mother asked.

"Sort of, along with Judge."

"Did you meet Sebastian Ryan?" she asked.

"I did, a real nice guy. He wants Hardie and me to help organize a group of kids to oppose the bypass."

Mrs. Boone was still smiling, and she was also watching Mr. Boone, as if she expected some harsh words. Theo wanted his mother around for this discussion.

Mr. Boone asked, "What sort of a group of kids?"

"Students at Jackson Elementary and also the soccer kids." Theo took a big bite as if such involvement was no big deal.

"That's a great idea, Theo," she said. "How do you plan to do it?"

"We haven't decided yet."

"Why do you insist on getting involved in this mess, Theo?" Mr. Boone asked slowly and firmly.

Theo's reply had been practiced a few times. He took a sip of water, cleared his throat, and said, "Because I think it's wrong for the Quinns to lose a farm that's been in the family for over a hundred years. It's wrong for the state to take private property for unnecessary projects. It's dangerous to build big roads next to schools and soccer parks, especially when no one has studied the pollution. It's wrong for politicians to help their buddies make money on stuff like this. Lots of reasons, Dad."

"And all good ones, I might add," Mrs. Boone said quickly as she glared at her husband.

Theo wasn't finished. "And most importantly, I'm ticked off at the men who hurt Judge. If you had been there when they tried to kill him, you might have a different attitude."

"Don't lecture me, son."

"I'm not lecturing anyone."

"He certainly is not," Mrs. Boone said. The battle lines were clearly drawn. Two against one. Mr. Boone was in the process of losing badly. She went on, "I think it's admirable that Theo wants to get involved in this fight. Most thirteen-year-olds could not care less."

Go Mom!, Theo thought as he cut another piece of chicken. You got him on the ropes, go for the knockout. But a truce came over the conversation and the Boones ate in silence.

Finally, Theo asked, "Dad, is it okay if I do this?"

To which his mother quickly responded, "Of course it's all right, Theo. You have some strong feelings about this, so go to work. Right, Woods?"

Woods Boone was in no position to argue, and he knew it. He surrendered with a weak, "I suppose."

Chapter 20

After lunch on Friday, Theo and Hardie took advantage of a one-hour study hall and met in the library. The school's Internet server was faster than their laptops, so they could save time by using the desktop models that were available to all students upon request. When they were properly logged in, and when the IT clerk disappeared, they quickly began searching for information. The soccer data was easier to retrieve than anything from the Stratten County School System.

The night before, after they had left the SEC offices (as full-blown activists), Hardie spent an hour on Facebook. He played for a team called Red United, affectionately known as RU, and RU had its own Facebook page. He searched other pages of other teams in the Under 14 division, and quickly put together a directory of about one hundred players, girls and boys. Tucked away in the library, Hardie roared through Facebook and added dozens of names to his list.

Theo hammered away at the school system. According to the official website, Jackson Elementary currently had 415 students in prekindergarten through fifth grades, but there was no listing of these students and certainly no information about them. There was a nice teachers' directory with color photos and e-mail addresses and such, and Theo decided this could be a valuable place to start. The Parent Teacher Organization (PTO) had a separate website with a few names and contact information but little more.

For almost an hour, the two were lost in their rambling searches for the names of people—students, teachers, parents, administrators—anyone who might be contacted with whatever Theo and Hardie decided to use in their little campaign.

After school, Theo was bored and killing time around the office. He planned to meet April Finnemore at Guff's Frozen Yogurt on Main Street at four o'clock, something they tried to do once a week. Her older siblings had fled an unhappy home, and April was often alone. Theo didn't feel sorry for her because she didn't want sympathy; plus, she was bright and funny and a gifted artist. He didn't consider her to be a girlfriend, not in the romantic sense, just a good friend who happened to be a girl. Most of his pals did not understand how it was possible to have a friend who was a girl but not actually a girlfriend. Theo had grown weary of trying to explain this. It was complicated.

Vince, the paralegal who worked for Mrs. Boone, popped into Theo's office and said, "Say, Theo, could you run these by the clerk's office and file them before five p.m.?" As he asked this question, he tossed down a folder filled with documents. It was probably papers in one of the many divorce cases Mrs. Boone had at the moment.

Theo jumped to his feet and said, "Sure. I'll go right now."

"Thanks," Vince said and disappeared.

There were few things Theo enjoyed more than a trip to the Stratten County Courthouse, and any excuse was good enough to make him hustle over there. He reached down, patted Judge on the head, explained he would be back shortly, then grabbed the folder and took off.

The courthouse was the largest building in town, and by far the most important. It had big, thick columns around the front entrance and long wide steps around them. Theo parked his bike at a rack and bounded up the steps. The main lobby was normally busy with lawyers, policemen, and clerks, but Theo knew from experience the place would be deserted late on a Friday afternoon. He'd heard his mother complain that it was impossible to find a judge after lunch on Friday, and he'd heard Ike tell stories of lawyers sneaking away to their favorite bars to recap another long hard week.

The lobby was deserted. Theo ran up two flights of stairs to the third floor, where Family Court was located. Inside, he found his favorite clerk of all, the young and gorgeous Jenny, the secret love of his life and a woman he would marry if she wasn't already married and pregnant.

"Well, hello, Theo," she said with a smile. Her soft blue eyes always twinkled when she smiled at Theo, and this always made him blush. He could feel his cheeks burning.

"Hi Jenny," he said. "Need to file these." He handed over the folder and she opened it.

"Great picture of you and Judge in the paper," she said as she went about her job of sorting out the papers. Theo just stood on his side of the tall counter and stared at her. "Thanks," he said.

"How's Judge?"

"He's doing great. Still banged up, but he'll survive."

"I hear those guys got out of jail this morning."

"That's right," Theo said. "Their lawyer finally got an appeal posted and got 'em out, but they're not finished. They'll spend some time eventually."

"I sure hope so," she said, stamping the papers as she shuffled them about. "I'll file these right away, Theo."

"Thanks Jenny. See you later." He should have turned around and started his exit, but, as always, Theo couldn't help but stare just a bit too long.

"Bye Theo," she said with yet another smile. "Take care of Judge."

"I will."

As Theo left the clerk's office, he realized his heart rate had increased. This usually happened when he was around Jenny. On the way out, he peeked into Judge Henry Gantry's courtroom, the largest and grandest of all, and was not surprised to see it dark and empty. He made his way down the stairs, looking at the massive oil paintings of dead judges. As he ambled through the main lobby, someone called out, "Hey Theo." He turned around and saw a face that was vaguely familiar, that of a guy in his forties with shaggy hair and a beard and battered sneakers.

"Norris Flay, with the *Gazette*," he said as he approached Theo. Flay was apparently one of those men who felt uneasy shaking hands with a thirteen-year-old kid, so he made no effort. He looked down, Theo looked up and said, "How you doing?"

"Fine. You?"

"Great."

"Got a minute?"

Not really. It was ten minutes before 4:00 p.m. and April would soon arrive at Guff's Frozen Yogurt, which was only a few blocks away. The son of two lawyers, Theo had been raised in an atmosphere of distrust when it came to reporters. Their job was to dig and reveal facts and details that people preferred to keep quiet. As lawyers, Theo's parents lived by a code of protecting, at all costs, the privacy of their clients. Theo was often amazed when he saw lawyers on television hotdogging it for the cameras as they blathered on and on about their clients and the details of their cases. Not so around good old Boone & Boone. His father was fond of saying, "Lawyers and cameras are a vile mixture."

"Maybe," Theo said cautiously.

"Did you like your picture in the paper yesterday morning?" Flay asked proudly.

"It was okay," Theo said, glancing around. "What's up?"

Flay glanced around, too, and a casual bystander might have thought a drug deal was taking place. "You leaving?"

"Yep," Theo replied.

"Good. I'll walk out with you."

They left the lobby, walked through the front doors, and stopped in the shadows of one of the columns. "How's the dog?" Flay asked.

"Fine." Theo had no idea why Flay would want to talk

to him, and the longer they were together the more nervous he became. What if someone saw them whispering in the shadows on the front steps of the county courthouse?

Flay lit a cigarette and blew a cloud of smoke above Theo's head. He was shifty eyed and a little jumpy, and Theo wanted to bolt.

"Look, Theo, there are a lot of rumors about this bypass and issues related to it. I have a source telling me a lot of local businessmen are pushing hard because they plan to make a buck, know what I mean?"

Theo was staring at his shoes.

Flay went on. "Especially the developers. Looks like they're a bunch of vultures just waiting for the bypass to get approved, then they'll swoop down and line both sides of it with shopping centers and fast-food joints. Before you know it, they'll have the bypass jammed up as bad as Battle Street, know what I mean?"

Nothing from Theo. Flay waited, blew some more smoke, then said, "The biggest crook might be a guy named Joe Ford. You know Joe Ford?"

"Never heard of him," Theo said, looking at Flay. It was a fib but Theo didn't care. He had met Joe Ford within the safe and secure offices of Boone & Boone. It was none of Flay's business.

Flay glared at him as if he knew the truth. "I doubt

that," he said. "Your father has been Ford's lawyer for many years."

"So?"

"So, now I hear Ford has fired the law firm of Boone and Boone. Why, well I don't really know, but I bet it's related to the bypass."

"What do you want from me?" Theo asked angrily.

"Information."

"Forget it. I know nothing."

"Perhaps you can learn something, do a little digging, find something that might prove valuable and help stop the bypass."

"Digging is your job, not mine."

"We're on the same side, Theo." Flay reached into his shirt pocket and whipped out a white business card. He thrust it at Theo and said, "Here's my phone number. You hear something, you give me a call. I swear it's all confidential. I have never revealed a source."

Theo took the card and walked away without saying a word. Though he was certain he'd done nothing wrong, it didn't feel that way. He got on his bike and took off down Main Street, wondering if he should tell his parents. Joe Ford had fired the Boone firm the day before—how did Flay know so soon?

At Guff's, April was waiting in their favorite booth.

She ordered her usual frozen yogurt, and Theo, his usual chocolate gelato covered in crushed Oreos. She was subdued, and Theo soon knew why. Her parents were in a constant state of war, and if they weren't in the middle of a divorce, then they were threatening to get another one started. Theo's problems vanished as he listened to his friend discuss the latest fights around her house. He could offer no advice, but he could certainly listen. April dreamed of running away, like her older siblings had done, but it wasn't possible. At the age of thirteen, she had no place to go. Trapped at home, she created fictional worlds to which she could get away. Her favorite dream was being a student in Paris, studying art and painting at the edge of the Seine, very far from home.

Theo worked his gelato and listened dutifully, though he'd heard of this dream quite often. He secretly hoped she would not tear up and start crying. She did not.

Chapter 21

Woods Boone was a lifelong mediocre golfer who had never had the time to sharpen his game with lessons or practice or more time on the course. When Theo was ten, his parents gave him a set of clubs for Christmas, and his father attempted to give him some free lessons. However, both soon realized that lessons, free or not, from a weekend hacker were not that valuable. So each year on his birthday, his father gave him a package of ten, thirty-minute lessons from a pro. Theo's swing improved dramatically, and by the age of twelve, he could almost beat his father.

Weather permitting, they played nine holes every Saturday morning at the Strattenburg Municipal Course, and followed this with a boys' only lunch, usually at Pappy's, a well-known downtown deli noted for its pastrami subs and onion rings. Though he enjoyed athletics, the doctors would not allow Theo to play team sports. Tennis was out, too. He could bike, hike, and swim and do almost everything else, but the doctors drew the line at team sports. This irritated Theo and had been the cause of much dismay and argument around the Boone home, but Theo was still on the sidelines. That's why he loved golf. With a few exceptions, he could play as well as anyone his age, though he had yet to prove this in tournaments. His father discouraged competition on the golf course. Mr. Boone believed golf was a difficult game to begin with and most people made it worse by keeping score, fooling with handicaps, gambling, and playing in tournaments.

But they always kept score. Not on the official scorecard clipped to the golf cart's steering wheel, but in their heads. Mr. Boone was usually seven or eight strokes over par for nine holes, and Theo was close behind. Both pretended not to know the other's score.

Mr. Boone was drinking coffee at the kitchen table when Theo came down with Judge. "We have a tee time?" Theo asked as he released Judge through the rear door.

"Nine forty-five," Mr. Boone said without looking up. "But, remember, Dr. Kohl wants to see Judge at nine a.m."

"I forgot," Theo said. "Can we still play?"

"Sure, but let's move it."

Theo and Judge ate quickly. Theo never showered on Saturday morning and that was another reason he loved the day. They tossed their golf clubs into the rear of Mr. Boone's SUV, and at nine a.m. walked into Dr. Kohl's clinic. He sized them up and said, "Headed for the course, huh?"

"We tee off at nine forty-five," Theo said, with some urgency in his voice. The course was always crowded on Saturday morning and being late caused major problems. While Mr. Boone waited in the reception area with yet another newspaper, Theo and Judge followed the vet to an exam room. Working quickly, but expertly, Dr. Kohl removed stitches, changed bandages, cleaned wounds, and reworked the splint on Judge's broken leg, and managed to do all this while talking to both Theo and the dog in a voice so soothing he could almost put one to sleep. In Theo's opinion, Dr. Kohl had saved the life of his beloved pet, plain and simple, and for that he would always be a hero.

Judge flinched and whimpered a few times, but he also realized he was lucky to be alive. He was a tough dog who could handle pain.

Dr. Kohl pronounced him "ready to go" and said he

should come back in a week. Theo thanked him again for saving Judge's life. "All in a day's work, Theo," he replied.

They stopped by the house, tucked Judge away, and headed for the golf course.

With its hills, ponds, abundant sand traps, and at least three treacherous creeks, the Strattenburg Municipal Course was difficult. But when you don't keep score, who cares?

Mr. Boone had been a bit aloof since the Joe Ford matter, and Theo sensed some lingering attitude. However, when his father parred three consecutive holes, the last with an impossible forty-foot putt, the attitude vanished and all was well. They played for two hours, and enjoyed the scenery, the fresh air, the good golf and the bad. They ignored the law, the firm, the bypass, and talked instead about the game. Mr. Boone had learned not to give advice or pointers to Theo while they were playing, but he was prone to say things like, "Now, Theo, I think Tiger Woods would use a sand wedge here and aim for the front lip of the green."

Theo suspected his father had no idea what Tiger Woods would do. They were in an entirely different world. Theo, though, had already learned that amateur golfers, even bad weekend hackers, often watch the pros on television and, because they're playing the same game, feel as though they are somehow connected.

He always listened respectfully to his father, then played the shot precisely as he wanted. So many times, when Mr. Boone was pondering a shot, Theo was sorely tempted to say something like, "Now, Dad, I think Tiger Woods would look at your ball and say there's no way you can put it anywhere near the green." But, of course, he said nothing.

There had been two or three occasions when Theo had matched his father shot for shot, and this had caused a slight but noticeable rise in Mr. Boone's stress level as they approached the last two holes. Regardless of how much he went on about how golf should be recreation and not competition, he really didn't want to lose to his son.

How can you lose, though, when you don't keep score?

Theo sensed this and sort of felt sorry for his father. Maybe one day when he was sixteen or seventeen it would be okay to win, but not at the age of thirteen. And not today. Mr. Boone made par on five of the nine holes. He had two bogeys and two double bogeys, for an unofficial score of 42, one of his better rounds. Theo played poorly and was happy there was no written record of the game.

They turned in the cart, loaded their clubs, changed shoes, and headed for Pappy's downtown and a pastrami sub.

That afternoon, Theo told his mom he was going to watch friends play soccer, and he would be home by 5:00 p.m. She asked a few questions, all of which Theo artfully dodged without being deceitful, then gave her approval.

At 2:00 p.m., as planned, Theo met April at the end of her driveway, and they took off on their bikes to the Stratten Soccer Complex. Normally, such a journey by bike would not be permitted. There were too many busy streets, too much traffic, and too much distance. The complex was 1.5 miles west of Battle Street, "out in the county" as folks liked to say, and too far for city kids on bikes. But, thanks to Hardie, Theo knew a few shortcuts and back roads. He and April rode furiously for thirty minutes, and when they passed Jackson Elementary School they were ready for a break. The complex was within view, its parking lot packed with vehicles.

Hardie was playing on field number six, and the game was in progress. Theo and April found seats in the bleachers and caught their breath. Hardie was a forward, and when the ball rolled out of bounds near the bleachers, he chased it and saw his two friends in the stands. He smiled and nodded, then hustled away. Theo and April watched a few minutes, got bored, and began wandering around. It was an amazing sight to see ten games in progress at the same time, all with fans screaming and coaches yelling and whistles blowing. The complex was in a beautiful setting, with hills on all sides, surrounded by woods and nature, far removed from any traffic congestion.

Why ruin it? Theo asked himself. Why slap a four-lane highway carrying twenty-five thousand vehicles a day through the middle of such a pretty, rural part of the county? Why choke up the place with traffic and smog? It made no sense.

He and April made their way back to the parking lot. Theo was holding his cell phone, and April was holding her mother's video camera. They began walking along a long row of parked cars, Theo on one side, April on the other, and as they went they videoed the license plates of the vehicles. No one else was in the parking lot; they were off cheering for their teams, but Theo kept an eye on the foot traffic. It wasn't illegal to video the license plates of a car anywhere, but he didn't want to be forced to explain what they were doing.

There were actually three large lots scattered around the complex, and it took almost an hour to walk behind every vehicle and record the license plate numbers. No one noticed what they were doing, though there were a couple of close calls. Theo simply put his phone to his ear and began talking.

They counted one hundred forty-seven cars and trucks. The plan was to review the video, write down the license plate numbers, go to the website of the DMV (Department of Motor Vehicles), and find a way to get the names of the owners. It was safe to assume, at least to Theo, Hardie, and now April, that the owners of the vehicles parked at the soccer complex could well be some of the strongest opponents of the bypass. What parent would want their kid playing soccer in an atmosphere of exhaust smoke and gaseous fumes?

Fortunately, the Red United team won, and Hardie's coach was in a good mood after the game. His name was Jack Fortenberry and his son was the team's goalie. According to Hardie, Coach Fortenberry was a soccer fanatic who coached teams in the complex during the fall and spring and also coached an elite travel team in the summer. Hardie had briefed him on the bypass and its dangers.

They met behind a net, far away from the others as the crowd was breaking up and leaving. Hardie introduced Theo and April to his coach, who quickly made it clear he had strong misgivings about the bypass. He distrusted the politicians, and he suspected a handful of big businessmen were pushing the project. He was angry that the proposed route ran next to the soccer complex, and he understood the potential hazards.

Coach Fortenberry said exactly what they wanted to hear. He offered to help in any way possible, so Theo laid out their plan.

Chapter 22

Judge, who was still sleeping on Theo's bed instead of under it, got restless on Sunday morning about the time the sun began peeking through the curtains. Theo always enjoyed sleeping a little later on Sundays, but that would not happen on this day. He told Judge to be quiet, and that made matters worse. The dog needed to go outside, and after fifteen minutes of harassing his owner, he won the battle. Downstairs in the kitchen, Theo said a lazy good morning to both parents as he carried Judge to the back door and released him.

"Why are you up so early?" his mother asked.

"Judge wanted to go out."

The kitchen table was covered with thick Sunday newspapers, and the way they were strewn about gave the impression his parents had been reading for some time. Theo glanced at the coffeepot and saw it was almost empty. He glanced at the clock—6:45. "You guys are up early too," he said.

"Couldn't go back to sleep," his father grunted.

"Who wants pancakes?" his mother asked. She didn't cook often, and Theo and Mr. Boone knew they should take advantage of every opportunity. "With sausage?" Mr. Boone asked.

"Of course."

"What kind of pancakes?" Theo asked.

"What kind do you want?"

"Blueberry."

"Blueberry it is." She was already opening the fridge.

Theo poured himself some orange juice and took a seat at the table. A headline in the *Strattenburg Gazette* caught his attention. It read: COMMISSIONERS UNDECIDED ON BYPASS. He picked it up and started reading. It was not written by Norris Flay but by another reporter. According to the story, two commissioners were in favor of the bypass; two "had problems" with it; and the fifth seemed hopelessly undecided. The loudest supporter was a Mr. Mitchell Stak, a fifteen-year veteran of the County Commission and its current chairman. Mr. Stak owned a hardware store south of town and claimed the bypass would not affect his business in the least. This appeared to be true. As a businessman, a retailer, he was described as a rabid pro-growth commissioner who had never voted against a new subdivision, shopping center, apartment complex, mini-mall, car wash, or anything else that might add to the area's "economic development." A conservationist described Mr. Stak as being a "terror to our clean air, clean water, and quiet streets." Stak fired back with a beauty: "The tree huggers would keep us in the dark ages."

The report went back and forth with the pros and cons, and it was obvious that hard feelings were developing and tensions were high. As he read, Theo noticed a knot forming in his stomach. Why was he getting involved in such a nasty fight? He was just a kid and this was a real war being fought by some hard-nosed politicians. Then he thought of Hardie and the Quinn family farm. He thought of Judge and the thugs who beat him.

He read on as the sausage began to sizzle in a skillet. His mother hummed in her bathrobe as she cooked away. His father was lost in the business section of the *New York Times*. Judge was whimpering at the back door, no doubt excited over the fresh aroma from the kitchen. Theo let him in.

The public hearing on the bypass would be held before the County Commission in just over two weeks, and from all indications it would be a regular brawl. Mr. Stak boasted that 75 percent of the people in the county were in favor of the bypass and his supporters would flood the public hearing with a massive show of strength. Hogwash, said Sebastian Ryan of the Stratten Environmental Council, the bypass is favored by a slim minority and most of those are business people who want to make a buck. The opponents would turn out in record numbers.

For the first time, Theo actually thought about going to the public hearing. It might be a cool thing to watch! Hundreds of angry citizens, all squaring off in front of the five county commissioners. It promised to be a controlled mob scene, probably with deputies scattered around the room to keep the peace. Theo doubted his parents would allow him to go, but he liked the idea. He decided to think about it and maybe ask them later.

Over pancakes and sausage, Mrs. Boone said, "Let's go to the early worship service."

Mr. Boone nodded and said, "Sure."

"I like it," Theo said. He really didn't have a vote in matters involving church attendance, but that rarely stopped him from offering his thoughts on the matter. The early service was more enjoyable. It ran from 9:00 a.m. to 10:00 a.m. and was not as stuffy as the main worship hour at 11:00 a.m. The dress was more casual and the sanctuary was not as crowded.

"Then you guys had better hurry up," his mother said. Theo and his father exchanged looks of polite frustration. It was just after 7:30. They had well over an hour to get ready. Mr. Boone could shower, shave, and get dressed in about twenty minutes. Theo, not yet shaving, could do it in fifteen. Both knew it would take Mrs. Boone at least an hour to get ready, yet she was telling them to hurry. But both remained quiet. Some things were not worth discussing.

After lunch, and long after church, Theo reluctantly went to his room to begin work on a book report. It was to be a three-page analysis of the main characters in Mark Twain's *The Adventures of Tom Sawyer*, one of Theo's favorite books. He liked the book but he didn't like the idea of spending a good chunk of Sunday afternoon writing about it. Nevertheless, he trudged up the stairs and closed his door. But he couldn't find the book. He looked everywhere, then went downstairs to the den and searched some more.

"Maybe you left it at the office," his mother said. Bingo! That's exactly where the book was.

"Be back in a minute," Theo said. He took off on his bike and ten minutes later slid to a stop at the rear door of

Boone & Boone. He unlocked it and stepped into the little room he called his office. He found the book where he'd left it, on a shelf next to his Minnesota Twins poster schedule.

Theo could not remember the last time he was all alone in the family's law office. The place was always busy with lawyers on the phone, clients coming and going, printers rattling away, Elsa up front running the show and directing traffic, and Judge sneaking around looking for either another nap or something to eat. Now, though, on a Sunday afternoon, there was not a sound. It was eerily dark and quiet as Theo eased through the hallway and walked to the front window by Elsa's desk. The conference room, with its dark leather chairs and book-laden shelves, was somber and still. Theo decided he preferred the place when there were people around.

The old wooden floors creaked as he headed back to his office. It had once been an old storage closet. To get there he always walked through two larger storage areas, filled with countless white cardboard boxes stacked neatly together. Things were changing, though. The digital age was dragging older lawyers like the Boones into the world of paperless files and storage, and not a minute too soon, in Theo's opinion. Why destroy so many trees to produce so much paper that becomes useless almost as fast as it is filed away? He'd had these discussions with his parents. At the age of thirteen, Theo was already a tree hugger.

There was a table where Dorothy and Vince placed files before they were officially boxed away for permanent storage. As Theo walked by it, something caught his attention. It was the name JOE FORD in bold letters on the side of a large expandable file. Evidently, Mr. Boone, having been fired by Joe Ford, was cleaning out his files and putting them away. This was somewhat unusual because Mr. Boone was notorious for leaving stacks of old files around his office for years after they were no longer needed. His brother Ike had the same habit.

Theo took a step closer and looked at the tabs in the Ford file. There was one labeled Sweeney Road. He knew better than to pry, but then Theo had a habit of being too curious, especially around the office. He opened the Sweeney Road file, flipped through a half inch of papers, and found what he thought he might find. The document was called an *option*—a rather simple title, and it gave the buyer the option, or the right, to buy two hundred acres of land from the seller, a Mr. Walt Beeson. Who was the real buyer? On paper it was an outfit called Parkin Land Trust (PLT), a corporation that had just been created and done so in a way to conceal the faces of the people behind it. Since the option he was holding came from one of Joe Ford's files, it was pretty obvious to Theo that Fast Ford had set up another company to hide behind.

Most documents regarding land and land transactions were required to be filed for public record in the county courthouse. Options, though, were not recorded, and Theo knew this. As he read on, it became clear the rumors were correct. Mr. Beeson would sell his two hundred acres near Sweeney Road to PLT if, and only if, the county commissioners voted to approve the bypass. At that time, PLT would pay Mr. Beeson the sum of $10,000 an acre, or a total of $2,000,000. If the county commissioners rejected the bypass, then PLT would owe Mr. Beeson the cost of the option, $50,000, and walk away.

There was a paragraph requiring both parties to keep the option as quiet as possible. Secrecy and confidentiality were crucial to the deal, which appeared on the surface to be a straightforward option. Nothing illegal. Developers like Joe Ford did their business by picking the next hot real estate spots and building on them. If they guessed right, they made a lot of money. If they guessed wrong, they lost a lot of money.

Theo wondered how Ike had learned of this deal, but he really wasn't surprised. Ike had a knack for hearing things around town. Theo kept flipping pages. The option was signed by Mr. Walt Beeson, as seller, and by a Mr. Frederick Coyle, a vice president of Parkin Land Trust. No sign of Joe Ford, yet. Under another tab, Theo noticed the words Parkin Land Trust, Inc., and he pulled it out. It contained the documents of the newly created PLT Corporation, a company Mr. Boone had put together only a month earlier. Theo scanned the documents, the office notes, even the handwritten scribble of his father, something he easily recognized. The new company had four owners, or stockholders: Joe Ford owned 50 percent; Frederick Coyle owned 20 percent; Stu Malzone owned 20 percent; and Peter Kyzer owned 10 percent. Theo had never heard of Coyle, Malzone, or Kyzer, and he quickly scribbled down their names. He placed the file in exactly the same position he'd found it, and hustled back to his office. If he needed to see it again, he knew where to find it.

He locked the rear door of the office and sped home. Upstairs, alone with Judge and with his door locked, he opened his laptop and began searching the white pages. He quickly found the addresses, phone numbers, and e-mail addresses of Coyle, Malzone, and Kyzer, all of whom lived either in the city or county. Theo searched Mr. Coyle and learned he had been sued by a business partner six months earlier. Theo made a note to check the file in the courthouse. A Google search of Mr. Kyzer produced a recent story in a local business magazine featuring him and his string of gas stations where an oil change cost $20 and could be done while you waited. He was forty years old and loved to fly helicopters and duck hunt, among other things.

There wasn't much to be found on Mr. Stu Malzone, but one brief entry from an old copy of the *Strattenburg Gazette* put icing on the cake. It was a wedding announcement two years earlier. Stu Malzone, age twenty-three, had just gotten himself engaged to one Belinda Stak, age twenty-one, daughter of Mr. Mitchell Stak. Both bride and groom were students at Stratten College. The engagement photo showed the smiling faces of two young people who looked younger than their ages.

Theo checked the white pages again to verify what he almost knew to be true—there was only one Mitchell Stak in Strattenburg.

His head was spinning as he tried to line up the facts and put them in order. Mr. Joe "Fast" Ford was secretly buying land to develop to make a killing when the bypass was built. To do so, he set up the PLT Corporation to hide behind. The five county commissioners would vote to approve or not approve the bypass. The loudest supporter of the five was Mr. Mitchell Stak. His son-in-law, Stu, now twenty-seven years old, had been given a 20 percent share of PLT by Joe Ford, and done so in a way that it would not be made known. On paper, a 20 percent share was worth $400,000, and that was before Joe Ford set about developing the land. It was safe to assume that the 20 percent share would be worth far more after Joe Ford leveled the property and covered it with motels, strip malls, fast-food joints, and parking lots.

Theo suddenly had a knot in his stomach, a thick, throbbing sensation that made him feel sick. He walked to his bathroom, splashed some water in his face, and said a few words to Judge, who seemed completely unconcerned.

An hour later, Theo was lying on his bed, staring at the ceiling, *The Adventures of Tom Sawyer* open and neglected on his chest. He hadn't been able to finish a single paragraph.

He kept thinking about his father. Woods Boone was a well-respected lawyer who took great pride in ethics and professionalism. He was scornful of other lawyers who cut corners and got into trouble. He served on Bar Association committees to promote proper behavior among lawyers. And on and on. How could his father be involved in such a shady deal? He had prepared the paperwork to create the PLT Corporation, and had represented Joe Ford for years. Mr. Boone had even supported the bypass during family discussions.

Theo admitted to himself there was a good chance his

father did not know Stu Malzone. In fact, he'd probably never met him. Maybe he had never met Mr. Coyle and Mr. Kyzer. Theo wanted to believe his father was working only for Joe Ford and doing what the client asked him to do. Theo clung to this belief, but he was still bothered by what he had discovered.

No crime had been committed; not by Joe Ford and certainly not by Mr. Boone. But something was wrong. If it was true that a close member of Mr. Stak's family would pocket a nice profit from the approval of the bypass, and if this were made known before the vote, then Mr. Stak would be humiliated and maybe run off the County Commission. Making it known before the vote might kill the bypass.

Theo knew, though, that he was in possession of information he wasn't supposed to have. Once again, he had sniffed through the secret files of Boone & Boone and allowed his prying eyes to see things that were forbidden.

Now what was he supposed to do? Maybe Ike would know.

Chapter 23

By the end of the school day on Monday, the little gang of activists had put together an impressive list of almost 400 kids who played soccer at the complex. Chase, the mad scientist and computer whiz, and sometime hacker, in the eighth grade, had been recruited to join the effort. Using the videos of the license plates taken by Theo and April the previous Saturday at the complex, the team made a list of all the cars, trucks, and vans. Meanwhile, Chase attacked the county's online vehicle registration records, and in less than thirty minutes had found his way into a file listing the names and addresses of all owners. These names led to a lot of kids' names.

Some names led to Facebook pages and e-mail addresses; others did not. Not immediately anyway. But the longer the activists toyed with their list, and tweaked it, and added to it, the more solid information they had.

Their plan was taking shape. They even had their own Facebook page and called it, "Bypass to Nowhere."

Unlike most of the mandatory Monday afternoon visits, today Theo really wanted to talk to Ike. Around 5:00 p.m., he left Judge at the office and raced away on his bike. Ike's office was only five minutes away from Boone & Boone, the firm he had cofounded twenty-five years earlier. That firm had prospered well over the years, while Ike was banished to the bush leagues with no license to practice law and little to do but prepare tax returns for people without a lot of money.

"How's my favorite nephew?" Ike asked as Theo fell into a rickety chair.

Same question every Monday. Theo, Ike's only nephew, replied, "Great, Ike, and how's everything in your world?"

Ike smiled and waved his arms around as if to say, "Look at my world. It's beautiful." It was not. It was cramped and dingy and depressing, and Ike's world was not a happy one. "Couldn't be better," he said. "You wanna beer?"

"Sure," Theo replied.

Ike reached into a small refrigerator partially hidden under a credenza and pulled out two drinks—a bottle of beer and a can of Sprite. Theo got the green one as Ike popped another top. Bob Dylan was singing softly in the background.

Ike took a long slurp and said, "So how's school these days?"

"School is a boring waste of time," Theo said. "I should be in college getting ready for law school."

"You're thirteen years old, not exactly college material. You'd look pretty silly walking around a college campus with a mouth full of braces."

"Thanks, Ike, for reminding me."

"Stick with the eighth grade for now. Straight A's still?"

"Close." The last thing Theo wanted was another painful discussion about his grades. He wasn't sure why Ike thought he had the right to pester Theo about his grades. "I met Joe Ford last week," he blurted, to radically change the subject.

Ike took another sip and said, "I'm sure that was a real thrill. Where?"

"At the office. He was there seeing my dad on some legal matter. He's the kind of guy who thinks talking to a kid is a waste of time."

"If Joe Ford can't make a buck off you, then he has no time for a little chitchat."

"Then he fired my dad. He got mad when he saw me and Judge in the newspaper vowing to fight the thugs who want to build the bypass."

"That was a bit strong."

"So. I was mad. And Dad got mad too when Boone and Boone lost such a valuable client. I'm not sure why our little law firm represents people like Mr. Ford, but I guess that's none of my business."

After a long pause, Ike said, "Look, Theo, I've never met Joe Ford. I guess I know some things about him, same as most folks in town. I doubt if he is a crook. Let's just say he's a typical businessman who's always looking for the next opportunity. That's the American way, right? And guys like Ford need lawyers, so there's nothing wrong with your father doing legal work for him. A law firm has gotta pay the bills, Theo."

"What if I saw something?" Theo blurted. "Around the office, some old files, you know what I mean, Ike?"

Ike glared at him. Theo's snooping around the office had caused problems in the past, and those problems usually ended up involving Ike. He asked cautiously, "Something to do with Mr. Ford and one of his deals?"

Theo just nodded.

"Something to do with the Sweeney Road property and the bypass?"

Theo just nodded.

"Something that I probably do not know about?"

Theo just nodded.

"Something that Fast Ford is hiding?"

Theo just nodded.

"Have you hacked into the firm's digital storage files again?"

Theo said, "No, and I wasn't snooping. I was minding my own business when I stumbled across some Joe Ford files someone had placed on a table to be retired."

Ike knew that Theo was rarely minding his own business around the law office. Ike slowly stood, stretched, rubbed his beard, then walked to a shelf and turned off the stereo. He leaned against the wall, folded his arms across his chest, and said, "Don't tell me anything else, Theo. The lawyer-client relationship is strictly confidential. Every client has the right to be protected—every current client and every former client. Those files are none of your business and you were wrong to look through them."

Theo suddenly felt lousy. He knew Ike was right, though he was not expecting such a sharp rebuke. But, Ike wasn't finished. "I don't care what's in those files. Theo, you have to forget about it. Am I clear?"

Oh *yes.*

"A lawyer has a duty to protect his client. Period."

"Got it, Ike."

Ike fell into his swivel chair and stared at his nephew. There was another long pause. Theo finally asked, "Should I tell my dad?"

"No. Just bury it."

"Okay."

Theo left a few minutes later. Riding slowly back to the office, he still could not accept the fact that his secret information would remain buried in a retired file, boxed away in the depths of Boone & Boone. It did not seem fair.

Chapter 24

After the final bell Tuesday, the activists hurriedly gathered in the school's auditorium. The room would be vacant for about thirty minutes, until rehearsal began for a sixth-grade production. Mr. Mount had bargained for thirty minutes on the grounds that his debate team needed some vague form of practice. They quickly arranged the stage to appear ready for a real debate, with a podium in the center and a long folding table on each side. Since it wasn't a real debate, chairs were moved in close and filled with fake spectators, a dozen or so friends drafted by Theo and Hardie. To improve the quality of the video, Mr. Mount used a camera on a tripod. When everyone was in place, Mr. Mount announced, off camera, "And now, Theodore Boone."

Theo stood from behind his table. To his right were Hardie, Chase, and Woody, all four wearing clip-on ties and bright-yellow surgical face masks. Theo walked to the podium and nodded to the opposing team, which consisted of Justin, Brian, Darren, and Edward, four other volunteers from Mr. Mount's homeroom. They, too, had bad clip-on ties and the yellow masks. The spectators, including April and some guys from Hardie's homeroom, were bunched together close to the podium. Their faces were also hidden behind yellow surgical masks.

Hardie's father had found the masks online. Nine bucks for a carton of fifty, available in every color imaginable.

Theo yanked his down and looked at the camera. With a frown he said, "My name is Theo Boone, and today the issue before us is the so-called Red Creek Bypass." He coughed twice, then covered his nose and mouth with the mask. Next to the podium was a large map of the county with the bypass highlighted in bloodred as if it were a deadly gash on the landscape. Theo pointed and said, "This bypass will take Highway 75 around the city of Strattenburg, out here into a more rural area, where it will destroy fifty homes, several farms, a hiking trail, a historic church, and it will bring about twenty-five thousand cars and trucks a day to the front door of Jackson Elementary School."

On cue, the spectators hissed and booed.

Theo continued: "It will also take out part of this soccer complex and cross the Red Creek River in two places."

More booing and hissing.

"The bypass will cost two hundred million dollars and is being pushed hard by businessmen, politicians, and trucking companies north and south of Strattenburg."

More booing and hissing.

"One of the worst aspects of this bypass is right here, at Jackson Elementary School, home to about four hundred students from prekindergarten through fifth grade. There has been no reliable study as to the noise and pollution near this school, but it's safe to say that the quality of air will be greatly harmed."

On cue, everybody started coughing, even the members of the opposing debate team. Theo, with great drama, said, "In short, this bypass is a bad project, a waste of money, a dangerous idea, and it should never be built." He stomped away from the podium as if ready for a fistfight.

The spectators managed to stop coughing and began applauding.

For the other side, Justin rushed to the podium, and from behind his bright-yellow mask said, "On the contrary, this bypass is needed so that some folks can make more profits. Trucking companies, land developers, construction companies—all of these and more will make huge profits. That's especially good for them, but it's also good for us."

A loud round of booing and hissing from the spectators.

"The more money they make, the more taxes they pay— well, some of them anyway—and the more taxes we rake in, the more stuff our leaders can do with it. Don't you see?"

The spectators did not see and continued their show of displeasure.

Mr. Mount stepped forward and said, "Okay, let's cut for a minute and rethink this."

The goal was a two-minute video, with the debate scene burning about thirty seconds. Under Mr. Mount's direction, they did another take, then another. On the third take, the two teams actually began yelling at each other, with names like "Liar!" "Crook!" and "Sleazebag!" thrown in for a bit of exaggerated drama. The spectators tossed debris at the podium while Justin ranted on.

With all faces hidden behind the surgical masks, it was easy to conceal the smiles and laughter. After half an hour, Theo, Hardie, and Mr. Mount were satisfied. They had enough footage for a great opening scene.

The filmmaking would become more difficult. For the second scene, many more actors were needed and there was a greater risk things could go wrong.

After school Wednesday, the activists met at an old soft-ball field not far from Strattenburg Middle School. Softball season was several months away and the field was supposed to be vacant that afternoon. However, in Strattenburg, as in most cities, no vacant field was safe during soccer season when coaches scoured the neighborhoods in search of any open area that might work for a quick practice. There had even been fights. The fine new soccer complex near Jackson Elementary was built to provide adequate space and thus reduce the pressure. It was packed five afternoons a week and throughout the weekend, but it seemed as though there would never be enough soccer fields.

But there was no soccer in sight, at least not of the organized variety. At precisely 4:00 p.m., bikes and cars arrived in a rush. Many of the players of Red United, Hardie's team, showed up and quickly began changing into their uniforms. Their coach, Jack Fortenberry, brought a bag of balls, some orange cones, a small, portable goal complete with netting, and some extra practice jerseys for the other "team." The other team was a ragtag bunch of nonplayers who'd been recruited by Theo and Hardie, most of whom came from their homerooms. In all, about fifteen players took the field, half wearing a Red United jersey, half wearing a white practice shirt, and all wearing bright-yellow surgical masks, as if the air was pure poison. Along the sidelines, parents held homemade signs that read: STOP THE BYPASS, PROTECT OUR KIDS, NO BYPASS GAS, and so on. The parents were also wearing the yellow surgical masks. Many of the adults were either Quinns or related to the family.

For extra drama, and perhaps a bit of humor, the two coaches, Mr. Fortenberry and Mr. Mount, strapped around their heads bulky gas masks of the World War I variety. They weren't real—Hardie had found them online for ten bucks each—but they looked authentic.

Theo was in charge of special effects, and after gauging wind directions, he and Chase eased down the foul line in right field. When no one was looking, they lit a smoke bomb, tossed it on the ground, and quickly got away from it. A slight breeze lifted the bluish smoke into the air and carried it over the field. Theo had done his homework. There was a city ordinance against the use of fireworks unless proper permission was granted, and Theo, of course, had chosen not to get permission. However, fireworks were defined as portable devices and objects designed to make loud noises when triggered. In Theo's opinion, the city's ordinance did not outlaw the use of silent smoke bombs. That's what Theo was prepared to argue, if, in fact, he got caught. Getting caught, though, seemed highly unlikely. Who was going to complain? Everyone at the site was on the same team, so to speak.

As a light fog settled over the field, the game began.

It wasn't really a game, but more of a playtime as the boys chased the ball around and kicked it as far as possible. They coughed and coughed, and gagged, and, under Theo's fearless direction, even collapsed in fits of wheezing as if overcome by diesel exhaust. Theo and Hardie filmed the fans, their signs, and the coaches trying to yell from under their gas masks. They filmed a penalty kick in which the goalie seemed to fall dead at the precise moment the ball blew by him.

The final scene was a pathetic shot of all the players lying on the field, all gasping and wheezing and unable to continue, much like dying soldiers left behind after a gun battle.

An elderly man from a nearby house showed up and began asking questions. "Where'd that smoke come from?" Everybody shrugged.

"You kids all right?"

More shrugging as the kids got up and began walking away.

"Should I call 911?"

"That's not necessary," Mr. Mount said.

"Why's everybody wearing a mask?"

"Air pollution," Theo replied as he hopped on his bike.

Saturday afternoon, the soccer complex was packed with ten games under way and cars wedged into overflow parking lots. Hardie had played that morning and was free for the afternoon. Theo, Chase, Woody, and April met him near the elementary school for the shooting of another scene. Because the driveway that led to the school also ran along farther to the soccer complex, there was a lot of traffic. They had to be careful. It was not a crime to wander across the campus of a public school on a weekend, but Theo did not want curious people asking questions. He knew from experience that security guards kept a casual eye on the various local schools during nights and on weekends.

The gang put on their yellow surgical masks and posed for photos by the large JACKSON ELEMENTARY SCHOOL sign near the front entrance of the campus, then they drifted behind the main building until they came to a playground. There was no sign of a security guard or school employee. Theo dropped another smoke bomb and walked away from it. Soon, there was a cloud drifting over the playground. While Chase worked the camera, Theo, April, Hardie, and Woody jumped into swings and began kicking and ripping through the air. At thirteen, they were too old to be posing as elementary school students, though the yellow surgical masks hid most of their faces. Shot from a distance, the scene just might work. Chase continued to back away with the video camera, and from fifty yards, he found his range. The scene became almost too good—kids on a playground, faces covered for protection as a cloud of dirty diesel exhaust settles over them.

"Perfect!" he yelled to his friends. "Just perfect."

Theo and Hardie slept over at Chase Whipple's Saturday night. The Boones and Whipples were close friends, and there was often a weekend sleepover in the works. The boys said they had a couple of movies to watch, but the real reason was to polish up their video. Chase knew of a website where they could purchase footage of almost anything imaginable, and for six dollars (paid for by Hardie's father and his credit card) they downloaded scenes of real eighteen-wheelers roaring along a crowded highway, exhaust pouring from their pipes. They downloaded shots of four-lane highways choked with slow-moving traffic. With Sebastian Ryan's permission, they borrowed footage, diagrams, and scenes from the Stratten Environmental Council's website.

Everything was loaded onto Chase's laptop, since he was the principal editor. Chase could do more with a laptop than anyone they knew. He had recorded albums, made movies, created comics, built science projects, illustrated stories, and had live interactive chats with kids from around the world. In the school's annual Computer Olympics, he had won the gold medal the past three years, often competing against kids three years older. If it was online, Chase could find it, and often before anyone else could find the On switch. And if the software existed, Chase could master it in minutes.

As they watched and brainstormed and sometimes argued, the video came together.

It began with a black screen and the loud noise of big truck diesel engines. The title *Bypass to Nowhere* appeared as the trucks grew louder offscreen. Cut to Theo, at the podium, introducing himself as he covered his nose and mouth with a bright-yellow surgical mask. As he railed against the bypass, the camera cut to the spectators, all wearing yellow masks, then to the other team. The audience booed and hissed as the debate raged on. The next scene, borrowed from the SEC, was a virtual ride along the proposed bypass. When the ride approached Jackson Elementary, the narrator, Sebastian Ryan, spoke gravely offscreen about the dangers to the students. Cut to a photo of the activists posing by the Jackson Elementary sign, all wearing yellow surgical masks. The sounds changed back to the roar of diesel trucks as the video changed to an action shot of the kids swinging happily on the playground while a dangerous fog settled over them.

The smoke bomb had worked perfectly, and the three boys were quite proud of themselves.

Suddenly there was the face of a young mother, wiping

tears and going on about the unknown dangers that 25,000 vehicles a day would pose to Jackson Elementary. She had two kids at the school. How could the county even think about such a project? Why not put the safety of the kids first?

The next scene was back at the debate, with Justin arguing the bypass was needed so more profits could be made. While the spectators booed and hissed, a couple actually tossed wads of paper at him. As he spoke, the video cut to a four-lane highway jam-packed with eighteen-wheelers and cars bumper-to-bumper.

The mock soccer game was the climax of the video. Chase cut and pasted until the scene was a mix of players trying to play while coughing and gagging in the toxic air, and parents watching and cheering behind yellow masks and hand-painted protest signs, and coaches trying to yell through bulky gas masks. When all the players had finally passed out, the final scene was a close-up of Judge, sitting in the bleachers, with a broken leg and a yellow surgical mask strapped around his face.

On the black screen were the words: PROTECT THE KIDS. STOP THE BYPASS.

After they watched it the second time, the boys couldn't suppress their laughter. If they could be forgiven for a bit of bragging, it was nothing short of brilliant, at least in their opinions. They tweaked it some more, cutting and adding a little here and there, and at 11:00 p.m., Mrs. Whipple stepped into Chase's room and announced it was time for bed.

Chase asked his mother if she wanted to see their masterpiece. Of course she did. Long ago, Mrs. Whipple had learned not to be surprised at anything that came from her son's laptop, most of which he kept hidden from his parents. But when he offered to give her a peek, she never said no.

For two minutes the boys held their breaths as their first viewer reacted. She smiled and frowned and even laughed when the soccer players keeled over.

"Very good," she said when it ended. "Excellent. Now what do you plan to do with it?"

"We're still discussing that," Theo said.

"I'll bet you are. Now go to sleep."

After she left the room, Chase sent the video to Mr. Mount and to Sebastian Ryan at the SEC.

Chapter 25

At 5:00 p.m. Sunday afternoon, Chase posted the *Bypass to Nowhere* video on their group's Facebook page (of the same name), and on YouTube as well. The page had over two hundred likes, and most began posting the link to the video. Sebastian Ryan sent the link to every other environmental group opposing the bypass, and they in turn e-mail blasted their members.

The last thing Theo did before turning off the lights Sunday night was to check YouTube. One thousand eight hundred eighty-three people had seen the video, including Theo's parents. While they seemed to approve, they were also worried about their son taking a public role in such a nasty political fight.

When Theo woke up Monday morning, over 3,000 had seen the video. When he arrived at school, his classmates talked of nothing else. By lunch, the number of viewers was over 4,000. By the time Theo bounded up Ike's steps for their weekly meeting late Monday afternoon, the number was almost 5,000.

Theo had e-mailed Ike the night before, and Ike had spent most of the day sharing the link with everyone he knew. He'd also read many of the comments. "Virtually all positive," he said. "Looks like you've really hit a nerve, Theo."

Theo, too, had read many of the comments and was overwhelmed by the responses. Most viewers were obviously opposed to the bypass and delighted to see the video attack it. Most admitted to laughing out loud at the soccer scene when both teams were overcome by toxic fumes. Not surprisingly, there were a few critics. One guy called the video a "two-minute cheap shot by a bunch of kids who don't vote, don't drive, don't pay taxes, and evidently can't read a newspaper." Overall, though, the video was being well received.

Ike wanted to know how they filmed it, and Theo told the story in great detail. He took credit for the smoke bomb idea, and he gave credit to Hardie for the yellow surgical masks. Ike loved the idea of including Judge, but made the observation that the dog looked fairly miserable with a mask.

They laughed for almost half an hour before Theo had to go. Neither thought of mentioning the secret information Theo had found in Joe Ford's file. Theo certainly had not forgotten it; he just didn't know what to do with it.

After the lunch break on Tuesday, Mrs. Gladwell, the principal, sent word to Theo that he was needed in the office. When Theo arrived, he saw Norris Flay of the *Gazette* waiting with his usual smirking smile. Flay had the habit of always looking as if he'd just rolled out of bed. His clothes were wrinkled, his hair a mess. He seldom shaved. Theo had seen homeless people downtown put together better than Flay.

"He says he wants to talk to you, Theo," Mrs. Gladwell said. They were standing in her office.

"We know each other," Theo said, eyeing Flay suspiciously.

"I'm working on a story about the video, Theo," Flay said. "It's a nice story, and I'd like to talk to you and your friends, the kids who made the video. It's kinda gone viral, don't you think? Ten thousand hits in the first thirty-six hours."

"It's doing okay," Theo said.

"It has created quite a buzz and that makes it news. That's why I'm here."

Norris Flay was everywhere, always sniffing around for some dirt, and occasionally for a good story. "What do you think, Mrs. Gladwell?" Theo asked.

"If I were you, Theo, I'd check with my parents."

"Good idea."

Theo stepped outside and called his mother. Mrs. Boone felt strongly that Theo had already received more than his share of attention in this matter. But, on the other hand, a rowdy fight led by a bunch of schoolchildren might turn the tide against the bypass. She cautioned Theo to watch his words, specifically not to use such favorites as "thugs" and "crooks." She also advised him to avoid answering any questions about the smoke bombs.

After school, Theo, Hardie, Woody, Chase, and April met with Norris Flay in an empty classroom, with Mr. Mount in attendance and listening to every word. Flay was obviously amused by the video—he even claimed to be opposed to the bypass—and asked easy questions. He admired their filmmaking talents, but was equally impressed by their knowledge of the issues. They had done their homework and knew more about the proposed bypass than some of the politicians he had interviewed. Hardie was very effective describing the total destruction of his family's farm and his grandparents' way of life. Theo knew more about eminent domain than some of the lawyers Flay had talked to. As always, Flay had his camera and took a few group shots. He couldn't predict when the story might run but felt like it would be soon.

At 6:30 the following morning, Theo awoke to his alarm and immediately went online to check the *Strattenburg Gazette*. He was stunned. The bold front-page headline announced: VIRAL VIDEO SHAKES UP BYPASS FIGHT. Under it were two photos. The first was a color shot from the video with the gang of activists posing at the Jackson Elementary School sign, all faces adorned with yellow masks. Under it was a photo taken by Norris Flay the previous afternoon. Their names were listed beside the bottom photo.

With a knot in his stomach, Theo quickly read the story, praying he had not been misquoted and said something that might get him sued in court. He had not. Flay did a nice job of describing the video, now with over 15,000 hits, and even included the link. He wrote that the video was causing a lot of trouble for the county commissioners, all five of whom were being flooded with angry phone calls, angrier e-mails, and even irate citizens who were showing up at the county offices and demanding face time. Flay had also visited Jackson Elementary and interviewed a few parents. One mother of four claimed to have seventeen registered voters in her extended family and not a single one would ever again vote for any commissioner who voted to approve the bypass. Another mother vowed to remove her two children from the school and pay private tuition. An angry father said he was organizing other families and raising money to hire lawyers to fight the bypass. A kindergarten teacher, name withheld by request, was quoted saying, "I'm shocked at the lack of concern for the safety of our children."

Not surprisingly, the only commissioner willing to talk was Mr. Mitchell Stak, who seemed as aggressive as ever. He claimed he had not seen the video but called it a "childish stunt" anyway. He welcomed the phone calls, e-mails, letters, and personal visits, saying, "This is what democracy is all about. I believe in the First Amendment, the right to free speech, and I urge all the people in my district to make themselves heard." He went on to tout the great advantages of the bypass.

Theo mumbled to himself, "And not a single word about your son-in-law making some big bucks if it's approved."

There was a soft knock on the door, then it opened. Mrs. Boone eased in and said, "Well, good morning, Theo. Couldn't wait to see the morning paper, huh?"

Theo smiled. Busted. "Morning, Mom."

"I made some hot cocoa," she said, holding two tall cups.

"Thanks, Mom." She sat beside him on the bed, Judge just inches away and looking for his own hot cocoa, and said, "Nice article, huh?"

"Very nice," Theo said. "I was nervous."

"Good. It's wise to always be nervous around reporters. But Norris Flay did a good job, I thought."

"Has Dad read it?"

"Oh yes. We've been discussing it in the kitchen."

"Is he upset?"

She patted his knee and said, "No, Theo. Your father and I are both proud. It's just that, let's say, we're concerned that you're in the middle of a fight that perhaps should not include kids."

"Oh really, Mom? What about the kids who go to school and play soccer out there? The kids who'll be forced to breathe the diesel fumes? What about the kids like Hardie, whose family will lose its property and other kids who'll lose their homes?"

Mrs. Boone took a sip from her cup and smiled at Theo. He was right, and she knew it. Still, he didn't understand how brutal the game of politics could be when the stakes were so high. "I didn't stop by to argue, Theo. Let's just say that your father and I are very protective."

"I know that, believe me I do."

There was a long pause as they stared at the floor. After he took a long sip, Theo said, "Mom, the public hearing is next Tuesday. I really want to be there. Is that gonna be okay with you and Dad?"

"Certainly, Theo. I'll be there, too. I'm opposed to the bypass and I want the commissioners to know it."

"Awesome, Mom. What about Dad?"

"He'll probably skip it. He doesn't like long meetings, you know?"

"Sure."

She left, and Theo followed her downstairs with Judge. He went through his morning ritual quicker than ever—shower, teeth, braces, clothes, and breakfast.

He couldn't wait to get to school.

Chapter 26

Late at night, with his bedroom door locked, Theo opened his laptop and began typing the letter. It was a letter he'd been thinking about for days, and though he seriously doubted he would ever mail it, he wanted to write it anyway.

Dear Mitchell Stak:

I have in my possession some papers that clearly show your son-in-law, Stu Malzone, owns 20 percent of a company called Parkin Land Trust. Joe Ford and two other men own the rest of the company. I also have a copy of a legal document called an option, which gives PLT the right to buy

two hundred acres from Mr. Walt Beeson near
Sweeney Road if the bypass is approved by the
commissioners of Stratten County. Looking at these
papers, it is very clear your son-in-law stands to
make a lot of money from the bypass. This is a
gross conflict of interest on your part. I have no
way of knowing what Joe Ford has promised you, if
anything, but I'm sure the newspaper reporters will
have a lot of fun digging through your trash. Here's
the deal: If you vote to approve the bypass next
Tuesday night, then I will hand over these papers
to Mr. Norris Flay with the Strattenburg Gazette.
If you vote against the bypass, then the slimy deal
between Joe Ford and your son-in-law will never be
mentioned, at least not by me.

Sincerely,
A Concerned Voter

After a lot of research, Theo had learned that it was
not against the law to send an anonymous letter. Anyone
can use the US mail to send a letter or a package to anyone
else without identifying themselves. And, as long as the
anonymous letter is not threatening, then the person who

sends it cannot be charged with a crime. Assuming, of course, that the person is ever discovered.

Was it against the law to threaten someone? Theo had struggled with this issue for hours. To commit a crime, a person making a threat must have the clear intention and the ability to carry it out. For example, if A threatens to kill B, but says so in a way that is harmless, then there is no criminal act. Likewise, if A threatens to kill B, and really means it, but is a quadriplegic stuck in a wheelchair, then he lacks the ability to carry out his threat. However, if A is dead serious and has the ability to make good on his threat, then the threat becomes a criminal act.

Such arguments were why Theo loved the law.

In the case of Mitchell Stak, though, Theo's threat of public exposure could not be considered a criminal act even if he were serious and could follow through. Why? Because exposing corruption is far different from killing someone. Exposing corruption is not illegal; murder, of course, still is.

Theo read the letter again and it made him even more nervous. He felt like David staring up at Goliath. Mr. Stak was a powerful politician who'd served on the County Commission for fifteen years, since before Theo was born. Who did Theo think he was, trying to intimidate such a man?

On the other hand, Theo would not get caught, at least

not in theory. If he in fact mailed the letter, he would do so in such a way that no one would ever know where it came from. That's the purpose of anonymous mail, right? The sender gets to hide behind a wall of secrecy. He would use rubber gloves and not lick the stamp. Everything would be typed, nothing handwritten, and he would print the letter at school, where it couldn't be traced. He would deposit it in a remote postal box, far from security cameras. He was certain he could pull this off.

Still, it did not feel right. It seemed kind of cowardly. There should be a better way to confront a crooked politician than by sneaking around firing off unsigned letters. But after three days of nonstop, hyperactive thinking and scheming, Theo had no other plan.

He turned off his computer, turned off the light, situated Judge at the foot of his bed, and tried to go to sleep. His eyes would not close.

The letter was a bluff and nothing more. It wasn't a real threat because Theo could never reveal what he knew. He could never show Norris Flay or anyone else the papers now stuck away in a batch of retired files deep in the storage boxes at Boone & Boone. Theo knew the rules. Ike had made them even clearer. When it came to a client's secrets, nothing left the law office.

So why not send the letter? What was the harm? It wasn't a crime. The Joe Ford files would be protected. Mr. Stak would read the letter, know immediately that whoever wrote it knew the truth, and at that point he might be terrified of being exposed. The anonymous letter stood a good chance of bullying Mr. Stak into voting against the bypass.

Was this right or wrong? Theo flipped and flopped for an hour as Judge glared at him in the darkness. Then he thought of something else: Wouldn't the letter reveal Joe Ford's business to Mr. Stak? Yes, it certainly would. But then, Mr. Stak already knew about the shady land deal, right? So the letter wouldn't reveal anything that Mr. Stak didn't already know. Would this be a violation of a client's secrets? "Maybe," Theo said aloud. "And maybe not."

The knot in his stomach was back, and he needed to use the bathroom. At midnight he was sitting in his bed, in the darkness, hunched over his laptop pecking away with some new ideas for the public hearing next Tuesday night. For the moment, the letter was forgotten.

He slept little, and at 6:30 got up and splashed water on his face. He turned on his laptop, and, as was his habit these days, went straight to YouTube. The bypass video had over

31,000 hits. Theo watched it again, a wide grin on his face. He then went to the *Gazette* and found another front-page story by Norris Flay. Evidently, Mr. Flay had ventured over to Jackson Elementary again and found a story about a teacher with a lot to say. Her name was Ms. Rooney, and she and her third-grade class had begun wearing yellow surgical masks as a sign of protest. This had quickly spread throughout the third grade, and the fourth, and there was a beautiful color photo of about fifty kids posing on the playground, all with the masks.

The yellow masks, a brilliant idea.

Below the photo there was another story about the bypass. The governor had passed through Strattenburg the day before to rally the troops and push for the project. He had spoken at a Business Forum luncheon and given his usual spiel about how much the area needed the bypass. There was a photo of him mugging for the camera with two of the county commissioners—Mitchell Stak and Lucas Grimes. He called both men "bold leaders" unafraid to make tough decisions.

Staring into the eyes of Mitchell Stak, Theo decided to mail his letter.

He waited until Friday afternoon. He had scoped out a mail drop-off box on a street corner near Gil's Bike Shop, a place he knew well. It was a typical large, blue metal US Postal Service box with a heavy pull-down slot at the top. As far as Theo could tell, there were no nosy video cameras on any of the nearby buildings.

He had three letters, all identical. The letters themselves were on plain white sheets of copy paper like a million found in every law office. The language had changed little since the original draft. The envelopes were plain white, too, but the wording was different. The return address was from a person who did not exist, a Mr. Toby Clemons, 667 Gorewood Street, Strattenburg. There was no such name in the phone book and no such street in town. Theo decided to use a return address to make the mailing look more authentic. One envelope was addressed to Mr. Stak at his home; another to his hardware store; and the third to the Office of the County Commissioners.

The mail was picked up at 6:00 p.m. each afternoon. At 4:10 Friday, Theo approached the drop box with the three letters in his backpack. He was a nervous wreck. Though he couldn't pinpoint exactly why, he felt as though he was in the middle of a serious criminal act. For almost a week, he had debated this back and forth, up and down, pros and cons, inside and out, and he had made his decision. What he was doing wasn't wrong. Maybe it didn't feel completely right, but it could not get him in trouble. And, most importantly, it might just kill the bypass, and save the Quinn family farm, and keep polluted air away from kids, and so on. Theo was convinced he was right.

Well, he'd been convinced at school, and at the office, and as he rode his bike over to the mailbox, but when he stopped and pulled the letters from his backpack, a voice told him not to do it. "Don't mail the letters. It's wrong and you know it. You're using secret information that you have no right to use. If you were a real lawyer, as opposed to a kid lawyer, you would be violating rules of ethics and could get into serious trouble. Don't do it, Theo."

His heart was pounding and his feet were heavy, and Theo knew he should listen to his conscience. The fact that something is not clearly wrong doesn't mean it's right. Ike had once told him that in court great lawyers always trust their gut. Right now, Theo's gut was turning flips.

He shoved the letters into his backpack and hurried away. After half a block, he felt much better. He was breathing, smiling, pedaling furiously, and his backpack weighed far less with the letters still buried inside.

Chapter 27

The last time Theo had been so excited before an event had been the opening day of the Pete Duffy murder trial. Then, his friend Judge Gantry had given Mr. Mount's class permission to sit in the balcony of his grand courtroom. The crowd had been standing room only— it was, after all, Strattenburg's biggest murder trial in decades—and Theo and his classmates were lucky to be there.

This, though, was far different. The public hearing was to begin at 8:00 p.m., and two hours before then groups were gathering outside the County Office Building. Near the large front doors, a line was forming of those wanting the best seats. Dozens of protestors with signs walked back and forth on the sidewalk near the street; it seemed as if all were opposed to the bypass. Two television crews were setting up.

When Theo arrived on his bike at 6:30, he met Hardie, Woody, Chase, and April, and they got themselves organized. They found a spot near a monument close to the front of the building, and began handing out yellow surgical masks to anyone who would take one. Hardie's father had bought a truckload and was there to help. In fact, the entire Quinn family showed up early.

There was a new wrinkle to their protests. April had the idea to include a yellow bandanna with the word TOXIC printed in bold black letters across the center. It was another brilliant move. She and her mother had found the material, and a screen printer donated their services. When properly attired, with yellow surgical mask and matching yellow TOXIC bandanna, each kid looked like a pint-sized terrorist. They soon attracted a crowd as every kid, and quite a few adults, pushed forward to get a free mask and bandanna. One of the TV crews took notice and began filming.

By 7:00 p.m., the small plaza in front of the building was swarming with hundreds of people, many of them kids adorned in yellow from the neck up. Traffic on Main Street was bumper-to-bumper and not moving. The doors finally opened and the crowd began to squeeze inside.

For public meetings, the commissioners met in a large auditorium with high ceilings and tall windows and rows and rows of cushioned seating. Down at the front of the room, the commissioners sat in five huge leather chairs with nameplates and microphones before them on a long table. A small army of aides and assistants were grouped behind them.

When Theo finally managed to get into the room around 7:30, all seats were taken and people were lining up along the walls. He found a spot to stand near the back, and as he took in the surroundings he was astonished at the sea of yellow. Hundreds of kids were there, and every one of them had a mask and a bandanna. Many of their parents did, too.

An administrator of some sort asked the crowd to be quiet. The commission was considering another matter and would appreciate some courtesy. Theo looked down, far away, dead center, and studied the frowning face of Mr. Mitchell Stak. He was the chairman, so he sat in the middle. All five, all white men, looked troubled.

The balcony was opened and soon filled. A fire marshal announced the room had reached its legal capacity and no one else could be admitted. Far across the room, Theo saw his mother. She, of course, could not recognize him because most of his face was covered in yellow and he had the word

TOXIC across his forehead, the same as several hundred other kids in the auditorium. Theo waved to her but she did not see him. Mr. Boone was not present.

The commissioners adjourned for a break and disappeared. The crowd bristled with nervous chatter and anticipation. It seemed as though the opponents outnumbered those in favor by at least ten to one, and it was difficult to believe the commissioners would have the guts to go against such a mob. Within a few minutes, the five commissioners returned, took their seats, and stared at the packed house. They were not looking forward to the next three hours.

Mr. Stak pulled his microphone close and said, "Good evening and thanks for coming. It's always refreshing to see our citizens involved in the issues of the day. We want to hear from you and hope we have enough time. According to our rules of order, we will conduct this public hearing in an orderly and civilized fashion. There will be no cheering, applauding, booing, hissing, or yelling. No form of public protest, other than what is available here at the podium. We will begin with the formal presentation of this project, commonly known as the Red Creek Bypass, and this will be done by various representatives from the State Highway Department. We, the commissioners, will have the chance to ask questions and lead a discussion. Following that, and time permitting, we will hear from our concerned citizens."

A group of men in dark suits stood up and circled the podium. A spokesman from the highway department introduced himself and began reading a long and boring introduction to the project. Ten minutes in, the crowd seemed to deflate as it became obvious this formal presentation might take forever. The first spokesman handed off to the second, an expert in traffic studies, and he soon buried them in a sea of numbers.

Adults struggle to pay attention to wearisome material. Kids have no chance. Theo was tired of breathing through the mask and absolutely numb with boredom. An adult behind him said, and not too softly, "They're trying to bore us to death so we'll go home. It's an old trick."

Another responded with, "Yes, that and starting at eight p.m. Should've started earlier."

There was quite a lot of mumbling throughout the auditorium. Kids fidgeted and left for the bathroom. When the third spokesman said, in a dull voice that never seemed to go up or down, "Now, the second traffic study is shorter than the first, and I'd like to go through it carefully," a wave of groaning went through the crowd. Occasionally, one of the commissioners would ask a question to break things up, but for the most part the spokesmen and experts for the state rambled on as if they might talk for hours. Nine p.m. came and went, with no end in sight. Maps and models were flashed onto large screens near the front of the room, the same stuff that had been in the newspaper and online for weeks. Nothing new.

The crowd was growing restless, but no one left. As bedtime approached for many of the kids, their parents seemed determined to stay. So what if they lost some sleep? This was far more important.

Tempers flared when Mr. Chuck Cerroni, the only commissioner to publicly condemn the bypass, began to argue with the highway department experts. This upset Mr. Lucas Grimes, a big supporter of the project, and the two commissioners engaged in several rounds of sniping at each other. Their anger and drama livened up the evening, but only for a few moments. When they finally settled down, yet another spokesman took the podium and began his part of the program.

It was almost 10:00 p.m. when the formal presentation finally ran out of gas. Mr. Stak leaned into his mike and said, "Thank you, gentlemen, for a very informative summary of the project. Now, we decided yesterday to allow one spokesman for the opposition to present a fifteen-minute rebuttal. I believe Mr. Sebastian Ryan of the Stratten Environmental Council will do that at this time."

The crowd, having survived two hours of misery, suddenly came to life. As Sebastian walked to the podium, a ripple of fresh energy went through the auditorium. He adjusted the mike and said, "Thank you, Mr. Stak, and thanks to the commission for allowing us to be heard." He paused, then dramatically, and loudly, said, "To put it frankly, gentlemen, this bypass is a rotten idea."

The room exploded with applause and cheering as hundreds of opponents finally had the chance to be heard. The crowd yelled and clapped with a burst of energy that startled almost everyone, most especially the five commissioners. Mr. Stak raised a hand and calmly waited for the racket to die down. He said, "Okay, that's enough of that. Please restrain yourselves. If you can't be quiet, then we'll ask you to leave." He was pleasant, wise no doubt from years of experience.

The crowd slowly settled down, but there was little doubt it was ready to rumble. Bored adults were no longer bored. Sleepy kids were wide awake. They listened intently as Sebastian Ryan began a point-by-point criticism of the bypass.

Every word he said made perfect sense, at least to Theo, who was thoroughly captivated with Sebastian at the podium. He was smart, calm, and with a beard and slightly longer hair was clearly the coolest speaker so far, in Theo's opinion. Sebastian was a lawyer who stayed away from courtrooms; instead, he fought to protect the environment. Theo had never thought about doing that kind of work, but at the moment he wanted to be like Sebastian. Though Theo felt a little ashamed to think such thoughts, he sort of envied Sebastian as the center of attention.

But not everyone was impressed. Mr. Lucas Grimes and another commissioner, Mr. Buddy Klasko, began firing questions at Sebastian. Everyone knew Mr. Grimes was in favor of the bypass, and as the evening progressed it had become clear that Mr. Klasko was too. Add the vote of Mr. Stak, the loudest supporter, and the bypass had three out of five, or a majority. A victory.

After half an hour of haggling and bickering, Sebastian Ryan began to lose his cool, and with good reason. Mr. Grimes and Mr. Klasko became even more aggressive in challenging every minor point. Mr. Cerroni, an opponent, tried to help Sebastian, and at times it seemed as if all five commissioners were arguing and pointing fingers. The crowd reacted badly with mumblings and groans and even a few boos that followed silly questions and comments.

Sebastian had been at the podium for almost an hour when things changed dramatically. During a brief lull in the arguing, a large and rather rough-looking man of about forty stood in the center of the auditorium and yelled, "Are you guys afraid to vote?" His sharp words cut through the heavy air and echoed around the auditorium. The crowd loved it and reacted with cheers and jeers. From somewhere in the rear a chant began, "We want a vote! We want a vote!" This spread instantly to all corners and within seconds hundreds of people were on their feet yelling as loudly as possible: "We want a vote! We want a vote!"

Theo was screaming it too and could not remember having so much fun.

Sebastian wisely sat down during this demonstration. Chairman Stak wisely let the crowd have its voice. After a minute or so, with the windows rattling, he slowly raised his hand and smiled. "Thank you," he said. "Please. Yes. Thank you. Now please be seated." The chanting stopped. Shuffling and grumbling, the people reluctantly sat down, or those who had seats did so. Theo and dozens of others had been standing for almost three hours.

Mr. Stak said, "Please, no more outbursts. Our rules of order require that we vote tonight, so please be patient."

Near silence in the auditorium. Mr. Stak picked up a sheet of paper, frowned at it, then said, "Now, according to this sign-up sheet, there are ninety-one people who wish to speak."

Many in the crowd exhaled. It was 11:05.

Mr. Stak continued, "Normally, when we have such a large crowd, we limit the speeches to three minutes each. Ninety-one speeches times three is about two hundred and seventy minutes, or four and a half hours. Not sure any of us want to say here that long."

Mr. Grimes interrupted by saying, "We can also change the rules if we want, right?"

"We have the power, yes."

"Then I suggest we limit the number of speakers."

This caused another argument among the commissioners, and for ten minutes they haggled about how to save time. Finally, Mr. Sam McGray, the oldest commissioner and the one who had said the least, suggested a limit of five speakers at five minutes each. That would guarantee the meeting would be over by midnight, and it would allow enough different voices to be heard. He said what everyone knew—that many of the speakers would say the same thing. The other four finally agreed and the rules were changed on the spot. Mr. Stak urged those who wanted to speak to huddle quickly with their friends and colleagues and decide who would say what. This caused some chaos and burned some more clock.

It was almost 11:30 when the first speaker stepped to the podium. He was a well-dressed gentleman from a business group and really wanted the bypass. Nothing he said was new; the congestion on Battle Street was choking traffic; Highway 75 was crucial to the rest of the state; economic growth depended on the bypass; and so on. Hardie's father spoke next, and, on behalf of the landowners sitting in the path of the new four-lane, delivered a lecture on the abuses of eminent domain. As a minister, he was accustomed to preaching, and he was very effective. A local plumbing contractor spoke in favor of the project because he employed eight crews with eight trucks and was frustrated with the slow traffic around town.

Theo was listening intently when he realized that Sebastian Ryan was beside him. Sebastian whispered, "Theo, take off your mask for a minute." Theo did so and said, "What's up?"

Sebastian, leaning down, unusually nervous, said, "Look, Theo, we think it's a great idea for you to speak on behalf of all these kids."

Theo's jaw dropped as a bolt of raw fear shot up and down his spine. He couldn't say a word. Sebastian continued,

"You'll be the last speaker, and when you walk down to the podium we'll get all the kids to follow you. It'll be a mob staring at the commissioners. You gotta do it, Theo."

"No way," Theo managed to say. His mouth was already dry.

"Sure, you can do it. We heard a rumor that the commissioners and a lot of other people want to see the kids who made the video. You're the man, Theo."

ach foot seemed to weigh a ton. As Theo walked down the center aisle, an aisle that led directly to the podium, and a few feet beyond that the hard faces of the commissioners, he realized he had nothing to say. Nothing was prepared. Not a single note. He was terrified, numb, having trouble breathing, and suddenly thinking of running away, of vanishing. A familiar face appeared to his left near the aisle. It was the Major, smiling proudly with a fist clenched, as if to say, "Go get 'em, Theo."

Theo was aware he was being followed; he could feel bodies hustling behind him and he could see the other kids moving in from his right and left. By the time he arrived at the podium, they were swarming around it. Dozens of kids, maybe hundreds, all in their yellow battle gear. Small kids from the kindergarten at Jackson Elementary, and older students from Theo and Hardie's band of activists. They bunched together in one yellow mob around the podium and looked at the commissioners.

Reluctantly, Theo stepped up to the podium. He took the microphone, pulled it down a few inches, and tried to think of something to say. The room was still and quiet. The rowdy mob of adults was silenced by the courage of the kids.

Theo tried desperately to remember all the rules and tips from his debating career, but at that horrible moment his memory failed him. He was as stiff as a board and had never been so frightened. After a few awkward seconds, it was obvious that no one was going to speak for him, so he cleared his throat, pulled down his yellow mask, and managed to say, "I'm Theo Boone, and I'm in the eighth grade at Strattenburg Middle School."

Mr. Cerroni came to his aid with a quick, "Are you the kid who made the video on YouTube?"

"Yes sir, with some friends."

This brought a roar from the crowd that stunned Theo. He glanced over his shoulder and saw people standing and yelling, and he managed to smile. At last count, the video had over 100,000 hits, and Theo guessed that everyone in the auditorium had seen it, and probably more than once.

When the moment passed and the crowd settled down, Mr. Cerroni said, "Well thanks, Mr. Boone, for that video." None of the other commissioners seemed to share his gratitude, but Mr. Sam McGray suddenly asked, "Are you the kid with the dog?"

"Yes sir."

"If I recall correctly, according to the newspaper, you referred to the people who want to build the bypass as a bunch of thugs, or something like that."

A few slight hisses from the crowd, good people behind Theo who didn't like the question. He realized he had the advantage of being a kid. The commissioners could not afford to be rude or rough with him. After all, he was only thirteen years old.

Theo replied coolly, "No sir. The thugs I was referring to were the thugs who beat my dog."

Mr. McGray nodded but said nothing else.

"How is your dog?" Mr. Cerroni asked.

"He's doing fine, thank you." There was a smattering of hands clapping.

"Can we move along?" Mr. Grimes said with great irritation. He was already tired of looking at all those brats out there, faces hidden behind yellow masks and bandannas.

Mr. Stak, as chairman, said, "You have the floor, Mr. Boone. No longer than five minutes." He glared at Theo, drilling him with his black eyes. Theo could not maintain eye contact. Theo could not breathe, or think, or do anything but stand, clutching the sides of the podium as the seconds ticked by and everyone waited. He felt like fainting.

One of Mr. Mount's more difficult sessions during debate had been the exercise in spontaneous speaking, or rising before a crowd with no notes, no preparation. Each side entered the debate cold, with no idea of what to expect, no idea of what the issue would be. Mr. Mount then announced the topic of the day, and each side was given five minutes to scramble, prepare, and try to form intelligent arguments. The first trick, according to Mr. Mount, was to relate the topic to something personal. Something you know a lot about.

Theo looked at Mr. Cerroni, an ally, and began, "Both of my parents are lawyers, and I'm lucky enough to spend hours in their office. I've sort of grown up there, and I've learned a lot, at least for a thirteen-year-old. I've done plenty of research into the legal rule of eminent domain, or the government's right to take property away from a person who doesn't want to sell. In our country, owning property is a very important right, something most Americans dream of, and for most Americans the dream comes true." He was breathing well. His voice was settling into a nice rhythm. He was still terrified but was managing to hide his fear. He remembered Mr. Mount's constant advice: "Speak slowly. Speak clearly. Speak deeply."

The crowd was silent. Go Theo.

"Eminent domain is to be used only in extreme cases. And this is not one of them. This bypass is not crucial to our lives here in Strattenburg. In fact, life will go on here just the same without the bypass. It might benefit a few, but the vast majority of us will never know the difference. So, under our laws, this project is not crucial. Therefore, the government cannot take property using eminent domain. And why should the government?" A slight pause for dramatic effect. He just remembered a great line—something he'd read in a Supreme Court case. "Just because the government is big enough, strong enough, rich enough, and powerful enough, doesn't mean it has the right to take land from its citizens."

This landed perfectly and the crowd reacted with another boisterous round of approval.

Theo had found his rhythm, his traction, and for a brief moment he relished being in the spotlight. He shifted his weight, like all good lawyers do in court when addressing the jury, and he wished he could pace, back and forth, but he was stuck behind the mike. He continued looking at Mr. Cerroni's friendly face and said, "You've already heard from Reverend Quinn, who described their family's farm. Well, I've been there. Hardie Quinn is my friend and one of the kids behind the video. He's grown up on the family farm, a beautiful one-hundred-acre piece of land that every one of us would love to live on. It has everything—thick forests for hunting, springs and creeks for fishing, the river for rafting, open pastures for growing hay, miles and miles of trails for hiking and horseback riding. There is a tree house, a barn, a stable, a toolshed, a cemetery, and an old country house where the Quinn family gathers every holiday and on most weekends. On the front porch, hundreds of Quinns have gathered over the years to drink iced tea and talk about life. In the backyard, they've had weddings, funerals, and a pig roast every Fourth of July. Imagine, just imagine, the State Highway Department reducing it all to rubble with a bunch of bulldozers. That would be wrong." Several in the crowd agreed and voiced their approval.

All five commissioners were staring at Theo, hanging on every word. He threw another punch with, "That would be an abuse of power."

He changed gears, raised his voice, and said, "Now, the

smart folks who designed this bypass think it's a good idea to reroute twenty-five thousand vehicles a day alongside an elementary school and a soccer complex. At least ten thousand of these will be large trucks with diesel engines. Since no one has bothered to conduct an accurate study of how much the air will be polluted, we don't, excuse me, you don't know what you're talking about. No one does. It seems to me though, and I'm a kid lawyer and not a kid scientist, that the last place you would want to build a busy four-lane road is right next to a school."

Hardie, Woody, Chase, and April were standing behind Theo, and on cue they began coughing and gagging. The rest caught on quickly, and for about thirty seconds the entire yellow horde shook and gyrated and bent double in an exaggerated display of the effects of diesel contamination.

Mr. Stak finally raised his hand and said, patiently, "Okay, okay." The coughing and gagging stopped immediately. The crowd was greatly amused, as were most of the commissioners and their assistants.

Theo continued, "Fortunately, my school is not close to the proposed bypass, but let me tell you a little about my school. In the past two months, my school has been forced to cut programs, lay off part-time workers, fire coaches, janitors, and cafeteria workers, and cancel trips.

Every school in our district has done this. Why? Budget
cuts. Not enough revenue. And it's not just the schools.
Our police and fire departments have laid off employees.
We've had cuts in street maintenance, garbage collection,
parks and recreation, in every single department. You know
that because you've been forced to cut the county's budget."
Another pause as he looked up for the kill. "How can you,
as leaders of our community, cut budgets one day and then
vote to approve a bypass to nowhere that will cost two
hundred million dollars?"

The crowd roared instantly and within seconds many
of those cheering were on their feet. The ovation went on
and on and gathered steam, and Theo took a step backward.
Mr. Stak raised his hand for order but he was ignored. What
was he going to do anyway? Arrest several hundred people
at one time? Wisely, he sat grim-faced and listened to the
roar. During one brief second, he locked eyes with Theo,
and both knew the truth.

Theo realized his little off-the-cuff speech had reached its
peak. Mr. Mount always said it's best to quit when you're ahead.
Many speakers lose their audience by going on too long. Plus,
Theo was so relieved to have made it this far, and he really had
nothing left. When the crowd finally settled down, he stepped
back to the microphone and said, "Thank you."

"Thank you, Mr. Boone," Mr. Stak said. It was almost midnight. The last speaker had just spoken. There was nothing left on the agenda but a vote on the bypass. It was obvious the crowd was not leaving until the commissioners voted. The kids in yellow did not return to their seats. Instead, they bunched even closer together around the podium and up the aisles, as close to the commissioners as they could get. They locked arms and sat on the floor.

"You guys can go back to your seats," Mr. Stak said, but the kids shook their heads. They weren't budging.

From the back, a loudmouth stood up and yelled, "We want a vote!" This immediately led to another deafening round of "We want a vote!! We want a vote!!" The walls shook and the windows rattled and the commissioners looked aggravated and confused. They wanted to huddle in a back room, as was their usual custom, and work out a deal before going public. But not tonight, not at this moment. There was nothing to do but vote.

Mr. Stak raised his hand again and finally brought the crowd under control. He said, "Very well, under the rules of this commission, it is now necessary that we take a vote. Madame Secretary, will you call the roll?"

At the end of their long table, the secretary said, "Certainly. All five commissioners are present and voting.

The vote will be a simple Yes to approve the bypass and No if you do not approve the project. Approval is by a simple majority. Mr. Stak?"

"Yes."

"Mr. Grimes?"

"Yes."

"Mr. Cerroni?"

"No."

"Mr. McGray?"

Mr. McGray was rubbing his white whiskers, troubled and deep in thought. With a scratchy voice he finally said, "No."

Theo was sitting on the floor in front of the podium, arm in arm with Hardie and April, and it seemed as though every kid around him was holding his or her breath. At that tense moment, things did not look good. The vote was tied 2–2, with only Mr. Klasko remaining, and he had given the clear impression he wanted the bypass.

"Mr. Klasko?"

Mr. Klasko's spine stiffened and his head jerked back. He ran a hand over his mouth, fidgeted, seemed to be short of breath, and finally managed to blurt, "Abstain."

Mitchell Stak and Lucas Grimes shot panicked looks at Buddy Klasko, who wasn't looking at anyone. He was gazing at a distant window, obviously wanting to jump through it. The crowd gasped and mumbled and no one seemed certain of the vote.

The secretary calmly announced, "By a vote of two in favor, two opposed, and one abstention, the motion to approve the Red Creek Bypass Project hereby fails for lack of a majority."

This set off a rowdy standing ovation. The kids in the front of the room were jumping and applauding. Their parents were hugging and high-fiving and shaking hands and celebrating. In the midst of the noise, the five commissioners gathered their papers and began to leave. The experts from the State Highway Department and the project's supporters grabbed their briefcases and materials and headed for the nearest door.

The meeting was adjourned, but the kids were not leaving. Instead, they swarmed around the podium, where Theo Boone stood in the center of the mob, soaking up his finest moment.

Chapter 29

The party began at 2:00 p.m. on the Saturday after the public hearing. It was thrown together at the last minute by the Quinn clan, all of them it seemed. They invited lots of people: neighbors whose land and homes had also been threatened, opponents who'd led the fight against the bypass, people like Sebastian Ryan and members of the Sierra Club, and many of the kids—the "yellow gang"—who had been so important in the fight. On a clear and beautiful afternoon, they gathered on the Quinn farm, behind the house, in the long, wide backyard where so many generations of Quinns had played and partied.

Hardie's grandfather, Mr. Silas Quinn, was in charge of his huge barbecue grill. It was covered with chickens, sausages, hot dogs, and ribs, and the thick, delicious aroma wafted over the farm. At times, the bluish fog from the grill reminded some of one of Theo's smoke bombs. Hardie's grandmother, Mrs. Beverly Quinn, fussed about the table where a feast was being assembled. Beans, coleslaw, casseroles, deviled eggs, corn on the cob—enough food for an army.

Theo was there with both parents and Judge, whose broken leg was now almost healed and not bothered by a splint. Judge romped around with a dozen other dogs. Woody, Chase, April, and several other friends flung Frisbees around while their parents drank iced tea and told stories about the great victory.

The party was nothing less than a celebration. The Quinns were truly thankful that their cherished land had been saved, and they expressed gratitude to everyone there. When it was time to eat, the crowd gathered around the table and Hardie's father, the Reverend Charles Quinn, led them in a long, lovely prayer. He gave thanks for almost everything, but especially for friends, old and new, who help others in a time of need.

With his head bowed but his eyes open, Theo looked down at Judge, who was hungry, of course, and said his own prayer of thanks.

Theodore Boone is faced with a number of dilemmas in this book. Some of the problems Theo confronts are listed below.

Do you agree with his choices?
What would you do in his place?

1. One of the themes of *Theodore Boone: The Activist* is expressed when Theo says 'the fact that something isn't wrong doesn't make it right.' What does that mean? Do you agree?

2. In the US, there's a debate about whether it's right to let the children of illegal immigrants attend school. Theo thinks they should. Why does he believe that? What do you think?

3. Percy is bitten by a copperhead, a type of poisonous snake, after teasing it. Theo is suspended as patrol leader because his troop leader thinks he should be held responsible for what happened to Percy. Do you agree?

4. In Theo's home town of Strattenberg, the Battle Street congestion is so bad it is hurting local businesses. Is it better for a town to have a bypass that damages the surrounding countryside and environment or to have polluting traffic jams in its centre?

5. Theo argues that compulsory purchase of people's homes and land to make way for things like bypasses is 'actually not such a bad law, because if the state can't take land when it needs to then nothing would ever be built.' Do you agree?

6. Hardie Quinn argues that the Boy Scouts have the duty to look out for nature and the outdoors, and the entire scouting handbook is filled with ideas about conservation and protection of the environment. He wants all three of the different scout troops in Strattenburg to get organized and fight the bypass. But the Troop Leader, Major Ludwig, disagrees because he thinks Boy Scouts should not be involved in politics. What do you think?

7. Mr Ford dismisses Theo's dad as his real estate lawyer after Theo publicly protests against the bypass. Is it right to sack someone just because they disagree with your views?

8. While looking through his father's private law papers, Theo discovers that a member of the planning commissioner's family will make a profit if the commission votes for the bypass to go ahead. He decides to write an anonymous letter to the commissioner telling him to vote against the bypass or risk having his secret exposed. Why do you think Theo decided to write the letter? Would you write the letter?

9. Ultimately, Theo decides not to send it. Why not? Do you agree with him? Or would you have sent the letter?

10. Is it right that Theo's dog eats everything BUT dog food?

How did you answer these questions?
Are you curious about how other people might answer them?

Well, now's your chance to have your say.

Join the conversation at facebook.com/JohnGrishamBooks and see what everyone else thinks.

Read where it all began . . .

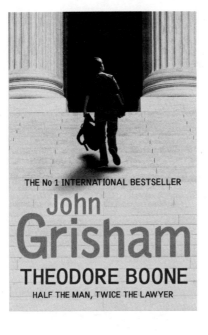

THE No 1 INTERNATIONAL BESTSELLER

John
Grisham

THEODORE BOONE

HALF THE MAN, TWICE THE LAWYER

HODDER &
STOUGHTON

Chapter 1

Theodore Boone was an only child and for that reason usually had breakfast alone. His father, a busy lawyer, was in the habit of leaving early and meeting friends for coffee and gossip at the same downtown diner every morning at seven. Theo's mother, herself a busy lawyer, had been trying to lose ten pounds for at least the past ten years, and because of this she'd convinced herself that breakfast should be nothing more than coffee with the newspaper. So he ate by himself at the kitchen table, cold cereal and orange juice, with an eye on the clock. The Boone home had clocks everywhere, clear evidence of organized people.

Actually, he wasn't completely alone. Beside his chair, his dog ate, too. Judge was a thoroughly mixed mutt whose

age and breeding would always be a mystery. Theo had rescued him from near death with a last-second appearance in
Animal Court two years earlier, and Judge would always be
grateful. He preferred Cheerios, same as Theo, and they ate
together in silence every morning.

At 8:00 a.m., Theo rinsed their bowls in the sink, placed
the milk and juice back in the fridge, walked to the den, and
kissed his mother on the cheek. "Off to school," he said.

"Do you have lunch money?" she asked, the same
question five mornings a week.

"Always."

"And your homework is complete?"

"It's perfect, Mom."

"And I'll see you when?"

"I'll stop by the office after school." Theo stopped by the
office every day after school, without fail, but Mrs. Boone
always asked.

"Be careful," she said. "And remember to smile." The
braces on his teeth had now been in place for over two years
and Theo wanted desperately to get rid of them. In the
meantime, though, his mother continually reminded him
to smile and make the world a happier place.

"I'm smiling, Mom."

"Love you, Teddy."

"Love you back."

Theo, still smiling in spite of being called "Teddy," flung his backpack across his shoulders, scratched Judge on the head and said good-bye, then left through the kitchen door. He hopped on his bike and was soon speeding down Mallard Lane, a narrow leafy street in the oldest section of town. He waved at Mr. Nunnery, who was already on his porch and settled in for another long day of watching what little traffic found its way into their neighborhood, and he whisked by Mrs. Goodloe at the curb without speaking because she'd lost her hearing and most of her mind as well. He did smile at her, though, but she did not return the smile. Her teeth were somewhere in the house.

It was early spring and the air was crisp and cool. Theo pedaled quickly, the wind stinging his face. Homeroom was at eight forty and he had important matters before school. He cut through a side street, darted down an alley, dodged some traffic, and ran a stop sign. This was Theo's turf, the route he traveled every day. After four blocks the houses gave way to offices and shops and stores.

The county courthouse was the largest building in downtown Strattenburg (the post office was second, the library third). It sat majestically on the north side of Main Street, halfway between a bridge over the river and a park filled with gazebos and birdbaths and monuments to those killed in wars. Theo loved the courthouse, with its air of authority, and people hustling importantly about, and somber notices and schedules tacked to the bulletin boards. Most of all, Theo loved the courtrooms themselves. There were small ones where more private matters were handled without juries, then there was the main courtroom on the second floor where lawyers battled like gladiators and judges ruled like kings.

At the age of thirteen, Theo was still undecided about his future. One day he dreamed of being a famous trial lawyer, one who handled the biggest cases and never lost before juries. The next day he dreamed of being a great judge, noted for his wisdom and fairness. He went back and forth, changing his mind daily.